The Franco-Czech novelist MILAN KUNDERA was born in Brno and has lived in France, his second homeland, for more than twenty years. He is the author of the novels *The Joke, Life Is Elsewhere, The Farewell Party, The Book of Laughter and Forgetting, The Unbearable Lightness of Being,* and *Immortality* and the short story collection *Laughable Loves*—all originally written in Czech. Like *Slowness,* his two earlier nonfiction works, *The Art of the Novel* and *Testaments Betrayed,* were originally written in French.

Praise for

Slowness

BY MILAN KUNDERA

"Audacity, wit, and sheer brilliance."
            —*New York Times Book Review*

"A playful envoi from a tender misanthrope; a rant set to music by Mozart."
            —Richard Eder, *New York Newsday*

"Rush to your bookstore for a copy—*Slowness* returns us to the pleasures of the dialectic, and to fiction which can be both entertaining and chock full of truths."   —*Baltimore Sun*

"Packed with ideas, laced with ridicule, *Slowness* (wonderful title) is a melancholy brief for mystery and anonymity."   —*Elle*

"Irresistible. . . . *Slowness* is an ode to sensuous leisure, to the enjoyment of pleasure rather than just the search for it."

—Cathleen Schine, *Mirabella*

"Coolly elegant . . . casually brutal . . . brilliant and oddly moving. . . . It embodies provocative thoughts on personal and social triviality from a postmodern master."

—*Publishers Weekly* (starred review)

"Dependably inventive and amusing, especially in its delicious sensitivity to the convolutions of contemporary self-consciousness."

—*Kirkus Reviews*

"Delightful. . . . [*Slowness* casts] serious light on the often absurd condition of our political and private lives in the late 20th century."

—*Dallas Morning News*

"An unconventional and witty *roman philosophique*... with [Mr. Kundera's] native playfulness and charm." —*Wall Street Journal*

"A nimble and witty fiction . . . *Slowness* combines literary past and imaginary present." —*Philadelphia Inquirer*

"Perhaps the happiest and funniest of Kundera's novels. . . . A book whose blessing is to believe in happiness, not only on the amorous but the political stage." —*San Francisco Chronicle*

"Paradoxically, *Slowness* . . . is the fastest-paced of Kundera's novels as well as the most accessible." —*Boston Globe*

Slowness

Books by Milan Kundera

The Joke

Laughable Loves

Life Is Elsewhere

The Farewell Party

The Book of Laughter and Forgetting

The Unbearable Lightness of Being

Immortality

Slowness

The Art of the Novel (ESSAY)

Testaments Betrayed, An Essay in Nine Parts

Jacques and His Master,
An Homage to Denis Diderot (PLAY)

MILAN KUNDERA

Slowness

Translated from the French by
Linda Asher

HarperPerennial
A Division of HarperCollinsPublishers

This book was originally published in France under the title *La Lenteur.*

A hardcover edition of this book was published in 1996 by HarperCollins Publishers.

First HarperPerennial edition published 1997.

Designed by Caitlin Daniels

The Library of Congress has catalogued the hardcover edition as follows:

Kundera, Milan
    [La Lenteur. English]
    Slowness : a novel / Milan Kundera ; translated from the French by Linda Asher.
      p.   cm.
    ISBN 0-06-017369-6
    I. Asher, Linda. II. Title.
PQ2671.U47L4613   1993
891.8'635—dc20   96-6253

ISBN 0-06-092841-7 (pbk.)

97 98 99 00 01 ❖/RRD 10 9 8 7 6 5 4

Slowness

1

We suddenly had the urge to spend the evening and night in a château. Many of them in France have become hotels: a square of greenery lost in a stretch of ugliness without greenery; a little plot of walks, trees, birds in the midst of a vast network of highways. I am driving, and in the rearview mirror I notice a car behind me. The small left light is blinking, and the whole car emits waves of impatience. The driver is watching for the chance to pass me; he is watching for the moment the way a hawk watches for a sparrow.

Véra, my wife, says to me: "Every fifty minutes somebody dies on the road in France. Look at them, all these madmen tearing along around us. These are the same people who manage to be so terrifically cautious when an old lady is getting robbed in front of them on the street. How come they have no fear when they're behind the wheel?"

What could I say? Maybe this: the man hunched over his motorcycle can focus only on the present instant of his flight; he is caught in a fragment of time cut off from both the past and the future; he is wrenched from the continuity of time; he is outside time; in other words, he is in a state of ecstasy; in that state he is unaware of his age, his wife, his children, his worries, and so he has no fear, because the source of fear is in the future, and a person freed of the future has nothing to fear.

Speed is the form of ecstasy the technical revolution has bestowed on man. As opposed to a motorcyclist, the runner is always present in his body, forever required to think about his blisters, his exhaustion; when he runs he feels his weight, his age, more conscious than ever of himself and of his time of life. This all changes when man delegates the faculty of speed to a machine: from then on, his own body is outside the process, and he gives over to a speed that is noncorporeal, nonmaterial, pure speed, speed itself, ecstasy speed.

A curious alliance: the cold impersonality of technology with the flames of ecstasy. I recall an American woman from thirty years ago, with her stern, committed style, a kind of apparatchik of eroticism, who gave me a lecture (chillingly theoretical) on sexual liberation; the word that came up most often in her talk was "orgasm"; I counted:

forty-three times. The religion of orgasm: utilitarianism projected into sex life; efficiency versus indolence; coition reduced to an obstacle to be got past as quickly as possible in order to reach an ecstatic explosion, the only true goal of lovemaking and of the universe.

Why has the pleasure of slowness disappeared? Ah, where have they gone, the amblers of yesteryear? Where have they gone, those loafing heroes of folk song, those vagabonds who roam from one mill to another and bed down under the stars? Have they vanished along with footpaths, with grasslands and clearings, with nature? There is a Czech proverb that describes their easy indolence by a metaphor: "They are gazing at God's windows." A person gazing at God's windows is not bored; he is happy. In our world, indolence has turned into having nothing to do, which is a completely different thing: a person with nothing to do is frustrated, bored, is constantly searching for the activity he lacks.

I check the rearview mirror: still the same car unable to pass me because of the oncoming traffic. Beside the driver sits a woman; why doesn't the man tell her something funny? why doesn't

he put his hand on her knee? Instead, he's cursing the driver ahead of him for not going fast
enough, and it doesn't occur to the woman,
either, to touch the driver with her hand; mentally she's at the wheel with him, and she's cursing me too.

And I think of another journey from Paris out
to a country château, which took place more
than two hundred years ago, the journey of
Madame de T. and the young Chevalier who
went with her. It is the first time they are so close
to each other, and the inexpressible atmosphere
of sensuality around them springs from the very
slowness of the rhythm: rocked by the motion of
the carriage, the two bodies touch, first inadvertently, then advertently, and the story begins.

2

This is what Vivant Denon's novella tells: a gentleman of twenty goes to the theater one evening.
(Neither his name nor his title is mentioned, but
I imagine him a chevalier.) In the next box he

sees a lady (the novella gives only her initial: Madame de T.); she is a friend of the Comtesse whose lover is the Chevalier. She requests that he see her home after the performance. Surprised by this unequivocal move, and the more disconcerted because he knows Madame de T.'s favorite, a certain Marquis (we never learn his name; we have entered the world of secrecy, where there are no names), the mystified Chevalier finds himself in the carriage beside the lovely lady. After a smooth and pleasant journey, the coach draws to a stop in the countryside, at the château's front steps, where Madame de T.'s husband greets them sullenly. The three of them dine in a grim, taciturn atmosphere, then the husband excuses himself and leaves the two alone.

Then begins their night: a night shaped like a triptych, a night as an excursion in three stages: first, they walk in the park; next, they make love in a pavilion; last, they continue the lovemaking in a secret chamber of the château.

At daybreak they separate. Unable to find his room in the maze of corridors, the Chevalier returns to the park, where, to his astonishment, he encounters the Marquis, the very man he knows to be Madame de T.'s lover. The Marquis, who has just arrived at the château, greets him cheerfully and tells him the reason for the mysterious invitation: Madame de T. needed a screen so that he, the Marquis, would remain unsuspected by the husband. Delighted that the ruse has worked, he taunts the Chevalier who was made to carry out the highly ridiculous mission of fake lover. Exhausted from the night of love, the young man leaves for Paris in the small chaise provided by the grateful Marquis.

Entitled *Point de lendemain* (*No Tomorrow*), the novella was published for the first time in 1777; the author's name was supplanted (since we are in the world of secrecy) by six enigmatic letters, M.D.G.O.D.R., which, if so inclined, one might read as: "*M. Denon, Gentilhomme Ordinaire du Roi*" (Monsieur Denon, Gentleman-in-waiting to the King). Then, in a very small printing and completely anonymous, it was published again in 1779, and it reappeared the following year under the name of another writer. Further editions appeared in 1802 and in 1812, still without the true author's name; after a half century of neglect, it appeared again in 1866.

Since then it was credited to Vivant Denon, and over this century, its reputation has grown steadily. Today it figures among the literary works that seem best to represent the art and the spirit of the eighteenth century.

3

In everyday language, the term "hedonism" denotes an amoral tendency to a life of sensuality, if not of outright vice. This is inaccurate, of course: Epicurus, the first great theoretician of pleasure, had a highly skeptical understanding of the happy life: pleasure is the absence of suffering. Suffering, then, is the fundamental notion of hedonism: one is happy to the degree that one can avoid suffering, and since pleasures often bring more unhappiness than happiness, Epicurus advises only such pleasures as are prudent and modest. Epicurean wisdom has a melancholy backdrop: flung into the world's misery, man sees that the only clear and reliable value is the pleasure, however paltry, that he can feel for himself: a gulp of cool water, a look at the sky (at God's windows), a caress.

Modest or not, pleasures belong only to the person who experiences them, and a philosopher could justifiably criticize hedonism for its grounding in the self. Yet, as I see it, the Achilles' heel of hedonism is not that it is self-centered but that it is (ah, would that I were mistaken!) hopelessly utopian: in fact, I doubt that the hedonist ideal could ever be achieved; I'm afraid the sort of life it advocates for us may not be compatible with human nature.

The art of the eighteenth century drew pleasures out from the fog of moral prohibitions; it brought about the frame of mind we call "libertine," which beams from the paintings of Fragonard and Watteau, from the pages of Sade, Crebillon the younger, or Charles Duclos. It is why my young friend Vincent adores that century and why, if he could, he would wear the Marquis de Sade's profile as a badge on his lapel. I share his admiration, but I add (without being really heard) that the true greatness of that art consists not in some propaganda or other for hedonism but in its analysis. That is the reason I consider *Les Liaisons dangereuses,* by Choderlos de Laclos, to be one of the greatest novels of all time.

Its characters are concerned only with the conquest of pleasure. Nonetheless, little by little the reader comes to see that it is less the pleasure than the conquest that attracts them. That it is not the desire for pleasure but the desire for victory that is calling the tune. That what first appears to be a merrily obscene game shifts imperceptibly and ineluctably into a life-and-death struggle. But what does struggle have to do with hedonism? Epicurus wrote: "The wise man seeks no activity related to struggle."

The epistolary form of *Les Liaisons dangereuses* is not merely a technical procedure that could easily be replaced by another. The form is eloquent in itself, and it tells us that whatever the characters have undergone they have undergone for the sake of telling about it, for transmitting, communicating, confessing, writing it. In such a world, where everything gets told, the weapon that is both most readily available and most deadly is disclosure. Valmont, the novel's hero, sends the woman he has seduced a farewell letter that will destroy her; and it is his

9

lady friend, the Marquise de Merteuil, who dictated it to him, word for word. Later, out of vengeance, the Merteuil woman shows a confidential letter of Valmont's to his rival; the latter challenges him to a duel, and Valmont dies. After his death, the intimate correspondence between him and Merteuil will be disclosed, and the Marquise will end her days scorned, hounded, and banished.

Nothing in this novel stays a secret exclusive to two persons; everyone seems to live inside an enormous resonating seashell where every whispered word reverberates, swells, into multiple and unending echoes. When I was small, people would tell me that if I set a shell against my ear I would hear the immemorial murmur of the sea. In that same way, every word pronounced in the Laclosian world goes on being heard forever. Is that what it is, the eighteenth century? Is that the famous paradise of pleasure? Or has mankind always lived inside such a resonating shell, without realizing it? Whatever the case, a resonating seashell—that's not the world of Epicurus, who commanded his disciples: "You shall live hidden!"

4

The man at the hotel reception desk is nice, nicer than people usually are at reception desks. Recalling that we were here two years ago, he warns us that many things have changed since then. They have developed a conference room for various kinds of meetings, and built a fine swimming pool. Curious to see the pool, we cross a very bright lobby, with great windows looking out onto the park. At the far end of the lobby, a broad staircase leads down to the pool, large, tiled, with a glass roof. Véra reminds me: "Last time, there was a little rose garden here."

We settle into our room and then go out into the park. The green terraced lawns descend toward the river, the Seine. It is beautiful, we are enchanted, we decide to take a long walk. A few minutes along our way, there suddenly looms a highway with speeding cars; we turn back.

The dinner is excellent, everyone nicely dressed as if to honor the times gone by, whose memory hovers beneath the ceiling here. Beside us are seated a couple with their two children.

One of these is singing loudly. The waiter leans over their table with a tray. The mother stares insistently at him, trying to get him to say something flattering about the child, who, full of himself from being looked at, stands up on his chair and sings still louder. A smile of pleasure appears on the father's face.

A magnificent bordeaux, duck, dessert (a house secret)—Véra and I chat, contented and carefree. Then, back in our room, I turn on the television for a moment. There, more children. This time, they are black and dying. Our stay in the château coincides with the period when, every day for weeks, they showed the children of an African nation whose name is already forgotten (all this happened a good two or three years ago, how could anyone remember all those names!), ravaged by a civil war and by famine. The children are thin, exhausted, without the strength to wave away the flies walking about on their faces.

Véra says to me: "Aren't there any old people dying in that country as well?"

No, no, what was so interesting about that famine, what made it unique among the millions of famines that have occurred on this earth, was that it cut down only children. We never saw an adult suffering on the screen, even though we watched the news every day, precisely to confirm that unprecedented phenomenon.

So it was completely natural that not adults but children should revolt against that cruelty of their elders and, with all the characteristic spontaneity of children, should launch the renowned campaign "The children of Europe send rice for the children of Somalia." Somalia! Of course! That famous slogan has brought the vanished name back to me! Ah, what a pity the whole business is already forgotten! They bought bags of rice, an infinite number of bags. The parents were impressed by this sentiment of planetary solidarity in their little ones, and they gave money, and all the institutions pitched in; rice was collected in the schools, hauled to the ports, loaded onto ships headed for Africa, and everyone could follow the glorious rice epic.

Immediately after the dying children, the screen is invaded by little girls six and eight years old, they are dressed like adults and have the appealing manner of aging flirts, oh it's so cute, so touching, so funny, when children act like adults, the little girls and boys kiss on the mouth, then comes a man holding an infant in his arms, and as he's explaining the best way to wash the diapers his baby just soiled, a beautiful woman approaches, opens her mouth, and sticks out a terrifically sexy tongue, which then penetrates the terrifically good-natured mouth of the baby-carrying fellow.

"Bedtime," says Véra, and she turns off the television.

5

The French children rushing to help their little African friends always remind me of the face of the intellectual Berck. Those were his glory days. As is often the case with glory, his was instigated by a defeat: let's remember: in the eighties of our century, the world was struck by the epidemic of a disease called AIDS, which was transmitted during sexual contact and which, early on, rampaged mainly among homosexuals. To stand up against the fanatics who saw the epidemic as a would be worth the risk; but in the third phase, an idea stopped him in his course toward the seropositive mouth: if he kissed a sick man too, that would not make him Duberques's match; quite the opposite, he would be reduced to the level of a copycat, a follower, a minion even, who by this hasty imitation would add still greater luster to the other man's glory. So he settled for staying put and smiling inanely. But those few seconds of hesitation cost him dearly, because the camera was there and, on the nightly news, the whole of France read on his face the three phases of his uncertainty, and snickered. Thus the children collecting bags of rice for Somalia came to his rescue at exactly the right moment. He took every opportunity to pelt the public with the fine dictum "Only the children are living in truth!," then took off for Africa and got himself photographed alongside a little dying black girl whose face was covered with flies. The photo became famous the world over, much more famous than the one of Duberques kissing an AIDS patient, because a dying child counts more than a dying adult, an obvious fact that at the time still escaped Duberques. But the man did not consider himself beaten, and a few days later he appeared on television; a practicing Christian, he knew Berck to be an atheist, which gave him the idea of bringing along a candle, a weapon before which even the most obdurate unbelievers bow their heads; during the interview he pulled it from his pocket and lit it; with the perfidious purpose of casting discredit on Berck's concern for exotic lands, he talked about our own poor children, in our villages, in our outer suburbs, and invited his fellow citizens to come down into the street, each carrying a candle, for a grand march through Paris as a sign of solidarity with the suffering children; then (suppressing his mirth) he issued a specific invitation to Berck to come join him at the head of the procession. Berck had a choice: either participate in the march, carrying a candle as if he were Duberques's choirboy, or else dodge it and risk the blame. It was a snare he had to escape by some bold and unexpected act: he decided to fly off straightaway to an Asian country where the people were in revolt, and there shout out loud and clear his support for the oppressed; alas, geography was never his strong suit; for him the world divided into France and not power but glory; his desire is not to impose this or that social scheme on the world (he couldn't care less about that) but to take over the stage so as to beam forth his self.

Taking over the stage requires keeping other people off it. Which supposes special battle tactics. The battle the dancer fights, Pontevin calls "moral judo"; the dancer throws down the gauntlet to the whole world: who can appear more moral (more courageous, more decent, more sincere, more self-sacrificing, more truthful) than he? And he utilizes every hold that lets him put the other person in a morally inferior situation.

If a dancer does get the opportunity to enter the political game, he will showily refuse all secret deals (which have always been the playing field of real politics) while denouncing them as deceitful, dishonest, hypocritical, dirty; he will lay out his own proposals publicly, up on a platform, singing and dancing, and will call on the others by name to do the same; I stress: not quietly (which would give the other person the time to consider, to discuss counterproposals) but publicly, and if possible by surprise: "Are you prepared right now (as I am) to give up your

19

April salary for the sake of the children of Somalia?" Taken by surprise, people have only two choices: either refuse and discredit themselves as enemies of children, or else say "yes" with terrific uneasiness, which the camera is sure to display maliciously, the way it displayed poor Berck's hesitations at the close of the lunch for the people with AIDS. "Why are you silent, Doctor H., while human rights are being trampled in your country?" Doctor H. was asked that question at a moment—in the midst of operating on a patient—when he could not respond; but when he had stitched up the open belly, he was overcome by such shame for his silence that he blurted forth everything one could want to hear from him and then some; after which the dancer who had harangued him (and here's another grip in moral judo, a specially powerful one) snapped: "Finally. Even if it does come a little late. . . ."

Situations can arise (under dictatorships, for instance) where it is dangerous to take a public position; for the dancer a little less dangerous than for others, because, having stepped into the spotlight, visible from all angles, he is protected by the world's attention; but he has his anonymous admirers who respond to his splendid yet thoughtless exhortation by signing petitions, attending forbidden meetings, demonstrating in the streets; those people will be treated ruthlessly, and the dancer will never yield to the sentimental temptation to blame himself for having brought trouble on them, knowing that a noble cause counts for more than this or that individual.

Vincent raises an objection to Pontevin: "Everyone knows you loathe Berck, and we're with you on that. Still, even if he is a jackass, he's supported causes we consider good ones ourselves, or, if you insist, his vanity has supported them. And I ask you: if you want to step into some public dispute, call attention to some horror, help someone being persecuted, how can you do it nowadays without being, or looking like, a dancer?"

To which the mysterious Pontevin replies: "You're wrong if you think I meant to attack dancers. I defend them. Anyone who dislikes dancers and wants to denigrate them is always going to come up against an insuperable obstacle: their decency; because with his constant exposure to the public, the dancer condemns himself to being irreproachable; he hasn't made a pact with the Devil like Faust, he's made one with the Angel: he seeks to make his life a work of art, and that's the job the Angel helps him with; because don't forget, dancing is an art! That obsession with seeing his own life as containing the stuff of art is where you find the true essence of the dancer; he doesn't preach morality, he dances it! He hopes to move and dazzle the world with the beauty of his life! He is in love with his life the way a sculptor might be in love with the statue he is carving."

7

I wonder why Pontevin does not make his very interesting ideas public. After all, he hasn't got such a lot to do, this Ph.D. historian sitting bored in his office at the Bibliothèque Nationale. He doesn't care about making his theories known? That's an understatement: he detests the idea. A person who makes his ideas public does risk persuading others of his viewpoint, influencing them, and thus winding up in the role of those who aspire to change the world. Change the world! In Pontevin's view, what a monstrous goal! Not because the world is so admirable as it is but because any change leads inevitably to something worse. And because, from a more self-ish standpoint, any idea made public will sooner or later turn on its author and confiscate the pleasure he got from thinking it. For Pontevin is one of the great disciples of Epicurus: he invents and develops his ideas simply because it gives him pleasure. He does not despise mankind, which is for him an inexhaustible source of mer-rily malicious reflections, but he feels not the faintest desire to come into too close contact with it. He is surrounded by a gang of cronies who get together at the Café Gascon, and this little sam-ple of mankind is enough for him.

Of those cronies, Vincent is the most innocent and the most touching. I like him, and my only reproach (tinged with envy, it is true) is for the childlike, and to my mind excessive, adoration he devotes to Pontevin. But even that friendship has something touching about it. Because they dis-cuss a lot of subjects that captivate him—philos-ophy, politics, books—Vincent is happy to be alone with Pontevin; Vincent brims over with odd, provocative ideas, and Pontevin, who is captivated too, straightens out his disciple, inspires him, encourages him. But all it takes is a third person turning up for Vincent to become unhappy, because Pontevin changes instantly: he talks louder and becomes entertaining, too entertaining for Vincent's taste.

For instance: They are by themselves in the café, and Vincent asks: "What do you really think about what's going on in Somalia?" Patiently, Pontevin gives him a whole lecture on Africa. Vincent raises objections, they argue, maybe they joke around as well, but not trying to be clever, just to allow themselves a little levity within a conversation of the utmost seriousness.

Then in comes Machu with a beautiful stranger. Vincent tries to go on with the discussion: "But tell me, Pontevin, don't you think you're making a mistake to claim that . . . ," and he develops an interesting polemic opposing his friend's theories.

Pontevin takes a long pause. He is the master of long pauses. He knows that only timid people fear them and that when they don't know what to say, they rush into embarrassing remarks that make them look ridiculous. Pontevin knows how to keep still so magisterially that the very Milky Way, impressed by his silence, eagerly awaits his reply. Without a word, he looks at Vincent who, for no reason, shyly lowers his eyes, then, smiling, he looks at the woman and turns again to Vincent, his eyes heavy with feigned solicitude: "Your insisting, in a woman's presence, upon such excessively clever notions indicates a disturbing drop in your libido."

Machu's face takes on its famous idiot grin, the lovely lady passes a condescending and amused glance over Vincent, and Vincent turns bright red; he feels wounded: a friend who a minute ago was full of consideration for him is suddenly willing to plunge him into discomfort for the sole purpose of impressing a woman.

Then other friends come in, sit down, chatter; Machu tells some stories; with a few dry little remarks, Goujard displays his bookish erudition; there's the sound of women's laughter. Pontevin keeps silent; he waits; when he has let his silence ripen sufficiently, he says: "My girlfriend keeps wanting me to get rough with her."

My God, he certainly knows how to put things.

Even the people at the nearby tables fall quiet and are listening to him; laughter quivers, eager, in the air. What is so funny about the fact that his girl wants him to get rough with her? It must all lie in the magic of his voice, and Vincent cannot help but feel jealous, given that, compared with Pontevin's, his own voice is like a flimsy fife straining to compete with a cello. Pontevin speaks softly, never forcing his voice, which nonetheless fills the whole room and makes inaudible the other sounds of the world.

He goes on: "Get rough with her . . . But I can't do it! I'm not rough! I'm too nice!"

The laughter still quivers in the air, and to relish that quiver, Pontevin pauses.

Then he says: "From time to time a young typist comes to my house. One day during dictation, full of goodwill, I suddenly grab her by the hair, lift her out of her seat, and pull her over to the bed. Halfway there, I let her go and burst out laughing: 'Oh, what a dumb lug I am, you're not the one who wanted me to get rough. Oh, excuse me, please, mademoiselle!'"

The whole café laughs, even Vincent, who is back in love with his teacher.

8

Still, the next day, he tells him reproachfully: "Pontevin, you're not only the great theoretician of dancers, you're a great dancer yourself."

Pontevin (a little abashed): "You're confusing concepts."

Vincent: "When we're together, you and I, and someone joins us, the place we're in suddenly splits in two, the newcomer and I are down in the audience, and you, you're dancing up there on the stage."

Pontevin: "I tell you, you're getting the concepts confused. The term 'dancer' applies exclusively to exhibitionists in public life. And I abhor public life."

Vincent: "You behaved in front of that woman yesterday the way Berck does in front of a camera. You wanted to draw her whole attention to yourself. You wanted to be the best, the wittiest. And you used the exhibitionists' most vulgar judo on me."

Pontevin: "Exhibitionists' judo, maybe. But not moral judo! And that's why you're wrong to call me a dancer. Because the dancer wants to be more moral than anyone else. Whereas I, I wanted to look worse than you."

Vincent: "The dancer wants to look more moral because his big audience is naïve and considers moral acts beautiful. But our little audience is perverse and likes amorality. So you used amoral judo on me, and that in no way contradicts your essential nature as a dancer."

Pontevin (suddenly in another tone, very sincerely): "If I hurt you, Vincent, forgive me."

Vincent (immediately moved by Pontevin's apology): "I have nothing to forgive you for. I know you were joking."

It is no mere chance that their meeting place is the Café Gascon. Among their patron saints, the greatest is d'Artagnan: the patron saint of friendship, the single value they hold sacred.

Pontevin continues: "In the very broad sense of the term (and in fact, there you have a point), there's certainly some dancer in every one of us, and I grant you that I, when I see a woman coming, I'm a good ten times more dancer than other people are. What can I do about it? It's too much for me."

Vincent laughs genially, more and more moved, and Pontevin goes on in a penitential tone: "And besides, if I am the great theoretician of dancers, as you've just acknowledged, there must be something they and I have in common, or I couldn't understand them. Yes, I grant you that, Vincent."

At this point, Pontevin turns from repentant friend back into theoretician: "But only some very small something, because in the particular sense I mean the concept, I'm nothing like the dancer. I think it not only possible but probable that a true dancer, a Berck, a Duberques, would in the presence of a woman be devoid of any desire to show off and seduce. It would never occur to him to tell a story about a typist he'd dragged by the hair to his bed because he had got her mixed up with someone else. Because the audience he's looking to seduce is not a few specific and visible women, it's the great throng of invisible people! Listen, that's another chapter to be developed in the dancer theory: the invisibility of his audience! That's what makes for the terrifying modernity of this character! He's showing off not for you or for me but for the whole world. And what is the whole world? An infinity with no faces! An abstraction."

In the midst of their conversation, Goujard comes in with Machu, who from the doorway says to Vincent: "You told me you were invited to the big entomologists' conference. I have news for you! Berck is going to be there."

Pontevin: "Him again? He turns up everywhere!"

Vincent: "What in God's name would he be doing there?"

Machu: "You're an entomologist, you should know."

Goujard: "For a year while he was a student he spent some time at the École des Hautes Études Entomologiques. At this conference they're going to name him an honorary entomologist."

And Pontevin: "We've got to go there and raise some hell!" then, turning to Vincent: "You're going to sneak us all in!"

9

Véra is already asleep; I open the window onto the park and consider the excursion Madame de T. and her young Chevalier took when they went out of the château into the night, that unforget-table three-stage excursion.

First stage: they stroll with arms linked, they converse, they find a bench on the lawn and sit down, still arm in arm, still conversing. The night is moonlit, the garden descends in a series of terraces toward the Seine, whose murmur blends with the murmur of the trees. Let us try to catch a few fragments of the conversation. The Chevalier asks for a kiss. Madame de T. answers: "I'm quite willing: you would be too vain if I refused. Your self-regard would lead you to think I'm afraid of you."

Everything Madame de T. says is the fruit of an art, the art of conversation, which lets no ges-ture pass without comment and works over its meaning; here, for instance, she grants the Chevalier the kiss he asks, but after having imposed her own interpretation on her consent: she may be permitting the embrace, but only in order to bring the Chevalier's pride back within proper bounds.

When by an intellectual maneuver she trans-forms a kiss into an act of resistance, no one is fooled, not even the Chevalier, but he must nonetheless treat these remarks very seriously, because they are part of a mental procedure that requires another mental procedure in response. Conversation is not a pastime; on the contrary, conversation is what organizes time, governs it, and imposes its own laws, which must be respected.

The end of the first stage of their night: the kiss she granted the Chevalier to keep him from feeling too vain was followed by another, the kisses "grew urgent, they cut into the conversation, they replaced it. . . ." But then suddenly she stands and decides to turn back.

What stagecraft! After the initial befuddlement of the senses, it was necessary to show that love's pleasure is not yet a ripened fruit; it was necessary to raise its price, make it more desirable; it was necessary to create a setback, a tension, a suspense. In turning back toward the château with the Chevalier, Madame de T. is feigning a descent into nothingness, knowing perfectly well that at the last moment she will have full power to reverse the situation and prolong the rendezvous. All it will take is a phrase, a commonplace of the sort available by the dozen in the age-old art of conversation. But through some unexpected concatenation, some unforeseeable failure of inspiration, she cannot think of a single one. She is like an actor who suddenly forgets his script. For, indeed, she does have to know the script; it's not like nowadays, when a girl can say, "You want to, I want to, let's not waste time!" For these two, such frankness still lies beyond a barrier they cannot breach, despite all their libertine convictions. If neither one of them hits on some idea in time, if they do not find some pretext for continuing their walk, they will be obliged, merely by the logic of their silence, to go back into the château and there take leave of each other. The more they both see the urgency to find a pretext to stop and say it aloud, the more their mouths are as if stitched closed: all the words that could bring aid elude the pair as they desperately appeal for help. This is why, reaching the château door, "by mutual instinct, our steps slowed."

Fortunately, at the last minute, as if the prompter had finally wakened, she finds her place in the script: she attacks the Chevalier: "I am quite displeased with you. . . ." At last, at last! Rescued! She is angry! She has found the

pretext for a contrived little anger that will prolong their walk: she has been frank with him, so
why has he said not a word about his beloved,
about the Comtesse? Quick, quick, this calls for
discussion! They must talk! The conversation
starts up again, and again they move off from the
château, along a path that, this time, will lead
them unobstructed to the clasp of love.

10

As she converses, Madame de T. maps out the ter-
ritory, sets up the next phase of events, lets her
partner know what he should think and how he
should proceed. She does this with finesse, with
elegance, and indirectly, as if she were speaking of
other matters. She leads him to see the Comtesse's
self-absorbed chill, so as to liberate him from the
duty of fidelity and to relax him for the nocturnal
adventure she plans. She organizes not only the
immediate future but the more distant future as
well, by giving the Chevalier to understand that
in no circumstance does she wish to compete with

the Comtesse, whom he must not leave. She gives him a short course in sentimental education, apprises him of her practical philosophy of love and its need to be freed from the tyranny of moral rules and protected by discretion, of all virtues the supreme virtue. And she even manages, in the most natural fashion, to instruct him how to behave the next day with her husband.

You're astonished: where, in that terrain so rationally organized, mapped out, delineated, calculated, measured—where is there room for spontaneity, for "madness," where is the delirium, where is the blindness of desire, the "mad love" that the surrealists idolized, where is the forgetting of self? Where are all those virtues of unreason that have shaped our idea of love? No, they have no place here. For Madame de T. is the queen of reason. Not the pitiless reason of the Marquise de Merteuil, but a gentle, tender reason, a reason whose supreme mission is to protect love.

I see her leading the Chevalier through the moonlit night. Now she stops and shows him the contours of a roof just visible before them in the penumbra; ah, the sensual moments it has seen, this pavilion; a pity, she says, that she hasn't the key with her.

They approach the door and (how odd! how unexpected!) the pavilion is open!

Why did she tell him she hadn't brought the key? Why did she not tell him right off that the pavilion was no longer kept locked? Everything is composed, confected, artificial, everything is staged, nothing is straightforward, or in other words, everything is art; in this case: the art of prolonging the suspense, better yet: the art of staying as long as possible in a state of arousal.

11

Denon gives no description of Madame de T.'s physical appearance; but one thing seems to me certain: she cannot be thin; I imagine her to have "a round and supple waist" (these are the words Laclos uses to characterize the most coveted female body in *Les Liaisons dangereuses*), and that bodily roundness gives rise to a roundness and slowness of movements and gestures. A gentle indolence emanates from her. She possesses the wisdom of slowness and deploys the whole range of techniques for slowing things down. She demonstrates it particularly during the second stage of the night, which is spent in the pavilion: they enter, they embrace, they fall onto a couch, they make love. But "all this had been a little hurried. We understood our error. . . . When we are too ardent, we are less subtle. When we rush to sensual pleasure, we blur all the delights along the way."

The haste that loses them that sweet slowness, both of them instantly see as an error; but I do not believe that this is any surprise to Madame de T., I think rather that she knew the error to be unavoidable, bound to occur, that she expected it, and for that reason she planned the interlude in the pavilion as a *ritardando* to brake, to moderate, the foreseeable and foreseen swiftness of events so that, when the third stage arrived, in a new setting, their adventure might bloom in all its splendid slowness.

She breaks off the lovemaking in the pavilion, emerges with the Chevalier, walks with him some more, sits on the bench in the middle of the lawn, takes up the conversation again, and leads him thereafter to the château and into a secret chamber adjoining her apartment; it was her husband who, in other times, had set this up as a magic temple of love. The Chevalier stops, dazzled, at the door: the mirrors covering all the walls multiply their reflections in such a way that suddenly an endless procession of couples are embracing all around them. But that is not where they make love; as if Madame de T. meant to head off a too powerful explosion of the senses and prolong the period of arousal as much as possible, she draws him toward the room next door, a grotto deep in darkness and all tufted in cushions; only there do they make love, lengthily and slowly, until the break of day.

By slowing the course of their night, by dividing it into different stages, each separate from the next, Madame de T. has succeeded in giving the small span of time accorded them the semblance of a marvelous little architecture, of a form. Imposing form on a period of time is what beauty demands, but so does memory. For what is formless cannot be grasped, or committed to memory. Conceiving their encounter as a form was especially precious for them, since their night was to have no tomorrow and could be repeated only through recollection.

There is a secret bond between slowness and memory, between speed and forgetting. Consider this utterly commonplace situation: a man is walking down the street. At a certain moment, he tries to recall something, but the recollection escapes him. Automatically, he slows down. Meanwhile, a person who wants to forget a disagreeable incident he has just lived through starts unconsciously to speed up his pace, as if he were trying to distance himself from a thing still too close to him in time.

In existential mathematics, that experience takes the form of two basic equations: the degree of slowness is directly proportional to the intensity of memory; the degree of speed is directly proportional to the intensity of forgetting.

12

Through Vivant Denon's lifetime, probably only a small group of intimates knew he was the author of *Point de lendemain*; and the mystery was put to rest, for everyone and (probably) definitively, only a very long time after his death. The work's own history thus bears an odd resemblance to the story it tells: it was veiled by the penumbra of secrecy, of discretion, of mystification, of anonymity.

Engraver, draftsman, diplomat, traveler, art connoisseur, sorcerer of the salons, a man with a remarkable career, Denon never laid claim to artistic ownership of the novella. Not that he rejected fame, but fame meant something different in his time; I imagine the audience that he cared about, that he hoped to beguile, was not the mass of strangers today's writer covets but the little company of people he might know personally and respect. The pleasure he derived from success among his readers was not very different from the sort he might experience among the few listeners gathered around him in a salon where he was scintillating.

There was one kind of fame from before the invention of photography, and another kind thereafter. The Czech king Wenceslaus, in the fourteenth century, liked to visit the Prague inns and chat incognito with the common folk. He had power, fame, liberty. Prince Charles of England has no power, no freedom, but enormous fame: neither in the virgin forest nor in his bathtub hidden away in a bunker seventeen stories underground can he escape the eyes that pursue and recognize him. Fame has devoured all his liberty, and now he knows: that only totally unconscious people could willingly consent these days to trail the pots and pans of celebrity along behind them.

You say that though the nature of fame changes, this still concerns only a few privileged persons. You're mistaken. For fame concerns not only the famous people, it concerns everyone. These days, famous people are in magazines, on television screens, they invade everyone's imagination. And everyone considers the possibility, be it only in dreams, of becoming the object of such fame (not the fame of King Wenceslaus who went visiting taverns but that of Prince Charles hidden away in his bathtub seventeen stories underground). The possibility shadows every single person and changes the nature of his life; for (and this is another well-known axiom of existential mathematics) any new possibility that existence acquires, even the least likely, transforms everything about existence.

13

Pontevin might be less harsh about Berck if he were aware of the troubles the intellectual recently had to endure from a certain Immaculata, an old schoolmate, whom, as a kid, he used to covet in vain.

One day some twenty years later, Immaculata saw Berck on the television screen, shooing flies from the face of a little black girl; the sight hit her as a kind of illumination. She instantly understood that she had always loved him. That very day, she wrote him a letter in which she recalled their "innocent love" of long ago. But Berck remembered perfectly that, far from being innocent, his love had been whoppingly lustful and that he had felt humiliated when she ruthlessly rejected him. This was in fact the reason why, inspired by the slightly comical name of his parents' Portuguese maid, he had at the time given her the nickname, at once sardonic and rueful, of Immaculata, the Unstained. He reacted badly to her letter (a curious thing: after twenty years he had still not fully digested his old defeat), and he did not answer it.

His silence upset her, and in the next letter she reminded him of the astounding number of love notes he had written her. In one of them he had called her "bird of night that troubles my dreams." That line, since forgotten, struck him as unbearably stupid, and he thought it discourteous of her to remind him of it. Later, according to rumors reaching him, he understood that each time he appeared on television, that woman he had never managed to stain was babbling at dinner somewhere about the innocent love of the famous Berck, who once upon a time couldn't sleep because she troubled his dreams. He felt naked and defenseless. For the first time in his life, he felt an intense desire for anonymity.

In a third letter, she asked him a favor; not for herself but for her neighbor, a poor woman who had got very bad care in a hospital; not only had she nearly died from a mishandled anesthesia, but she was being refused the slightest compensation. If Berck went to such pains for African children, let him prove he could take some interest in ordinary people in his own country, even if they didn't give him an opportunity for strutting on television.

Then the woman herself wrote him, using

Immaculata as her reference: ". . . you remember, monsieur, the young girl whom you wrote that she was your immaculate virgin who troubled your nights." Was it possible? Was it possible? Dashing from one end of his apartment to the other, Berck howled and raged. He tore up the letter, spat on it, and flung it into the garbage.

One day, he learned from the chief of a television channel that a woman producer wanted to do a profile of him. With irritation, he then remembered the ironical remark about his interest in strutting on television, for the producer who wanted to film him was the bird of night herself, Immaculata in person! A vexing situation: in principle, he considered the proposal to do a film on him an excellent thing because he had always hoped to transform his life into a work of art; but until that moment it had never occurred to him that such a work could be a comedy! With that danger suddenly revealed, he determined to keep Immaculata as far away as possible from his life and begged the chief (who was thoroughly astounded by his modesty) to put off the project, as it was premature for someone so young and unimportant as himself.

14

This story reminds me of another I happen to know, because of the library that covers every wall of Goujard's apartment. Once, when I was venting my spleen to him, he showed me a shelf bearing a sign in his own hand: "Masterpieces of Unintentional Humor," and with an evil smile, he pulled out a book a woman journalist had published, in 1972, on her love for Kissinger, if you still recall the name of the most famous political figure of that time, adviser to President Nixon and architect of the peace between the United States and Vietnam.

This is the story: she meets with Kissinger in Washington to interview him, first for a magazine, then for television. They have several sessions but never breach the bounds of strictly professional relations: one or two dinners to prepare the broadcast, a few visits to his office in the White House and to his home, alone and then surrounded by a crew, and so on. Bit by bit, Kissinger takes a dislike to her. He's no fool, he knows what's going on, and to keep her at a distance he offers a few eloquent observations on how women are drawn to power and on how his position requires him to forgo any personal life.

With touching sincerity, she reports all these evasions, which, by the way, do not discourage her, given her unshakable conviction that the two of them are meant for each other. Does he seem guarded and mistrustful? that does not surprise her: she has strong views on the horrible women he has known before; she is sure that once he understands how much she loves him, he will forget his worries, relax his guard. Ah, she is so sure of the purity of her love! She could swear to it: there is absolutely no question of erotic obsession on her part. "Sexually, he left me cold," she writes, and several times she repeats (with an odd motherly sadism) that he dresses badly; that he is not handsome; that he has poor taste in women; "he must be a poor lover," she adjudges, even as she proclaims she loves him all the more for that. She has two children, so does he, she lays plans—he has no idea—for joint vacations on the Côte d'Azur and is delighted that the two little Kissingers can thus learn French in a pleasant way.

One day, she sends her camera crew to shoot Kissinger's apartment, and no longer able to contain himself, he sends them packing like a bunch of trespassers. On another occasion, he calls her into his office and, his voice exceptionally stern and chill, tells her he will no longer stand for her ambiguous behavior with him. At first she is in deep despair. But very soon she begins to say to herself: no doubt about it, she is considered politically dangerous and Kissinger has been told by counterespionage to stop seeing her; the office where they meet is bristling with microphones and he knows it; his so astoundingly cruel remarks are meant not for her but for the invisible cops monitoring them. She gazes at him with an understanding and melancholy smile; the scene seems to her lit by tragic (the adjective she uses constantly) beauty: he is forced to deal her these blows, and meanwhile his gaze speaks to her of love.

Goujard is laughing, but I tell him: the obvious truth of the actual situation visible through the woman's fantasy is less important than he thinks; that's just a paltry, literal truth, it pales in the face of another one, which is loftier and timeless:

the truth of the Book. Even in her first encounter with her idol, this book was sitting in majesty, invisible, on a little table between them, being from that moment forward the unacknowledged and unconscious objective of her whole adventure. Book? What for? To lay out a portrait of Kissinger? Not at all, she had absolutely nothing to say about him! What fascinated her was her own truth about herself. She did not want Kissinger, still less his body ("he must be a poor lover"); she wanted to amplify her self, bring it out of the narrow circle of her life, make it blaze, turn it into light. Kissinger was for her a mythological steed, a winged horse that her self would mount for her great flight across the sky.

"She was a fool," Goujard concludes curtly, scoffing at my fancy analyses.

"No, no," I say, "witnesses attest to her intelligence. It's something different from stupidity. She was convinced she was among the elect."

15

Being among the elect is a theological notion that means: not as a matter of merit but by a supernatural judgment, a free, even capricious, determination of God, a person is chosen for something exceptional and extraordinary. From such a conviction the saints drew the strength to withstand the most dreadful tortures. Like parodies of themselves, theological notions are reflected in the triviality of our lives; each of us suffers (more or less) from the baseness of his too commonplace life and yearns to escape it and rise to a higher level. All of us have known the illusion (more or less strong) that we are worthy of that higher level, that we are predestined and chosen for it.

The feeling of being elect is present, for instance, in every love relation. For love is by definition an unmerited gift; being loved without meriting it is the very proof of real love. If a woman tells me: I love you because you're intelligent, because you're decent, because you buy me gifts, because you don't chase women, because you do the dishes, then I'm disappointed; such love seems a rather self-interested business. How much finer it is to hear: I'm crazy about you even though you're neither intelligent nor decent, even though you're a liar, an egotist, a bastard.

Perhaps it is as an infant that one first experiences the illusion of being elect, because of the maternal attentions one receives without meriting them and demands with all the more determination. Upbringing should get rid of that illusion and make clear that everything in life has a price. But it is often too late. You have surely seen some ten-year-old girl who is trying to impose her will on her little friends and who, suddenly finding herself short of arguments, shouts with astounding arrogance: "Because I say so"; or: "Because that's how I want it." She feels elect. But one day she is going to say "Because that's how I want it," and everyone around her will burst out laughing. When a person sees himself as elect, what can he do to prove his election, to make himself and others believe that he does not belong to the common herd?

That is where the era founded on the invention of photography comes to the rescue, with its stars, its dancers, its celebrities, whose images, projected onto an enormous screen, are visible from afar by all, are admired by all, and are to all beyond reach. Through a worshipful fixation on famous people, a person who sees himself as elect serves public notice of both his membership in the extraordinary and his distance from the ordinary, which is to say, in concrete terms, from the neighbors, the colleagues, the partners, with whom he (or she) is obliged to live.

Thus famous people have become a public resource like sewer systems, like Social Security, like insurance, like insane asylums. But they are useful only on condition of remaining truly beyond reach. When someone seeks to confirm his elect status by a direct, personal contact with someone famous, he runs the risk of being thrown out, like the woman who loved Kissinger. In theological language, that is called the Fall. That is why in her book the woman who loved Kissinger describes her love explicitly, and correctly, as "tragic," because a fall, despite Goujard's jeers, is tragic by definition.

Until the moment she realized she was in love with Berck, Immaculata had lived the life most women live: a few marriages, a few divorces, a few lovers who brought her a disappointment as regular as it was tranquil and almost agreeable. The latest of her lovers is particularly worshipful; she finds him somewhat more bearable than the others, not only because he is submissive but because he is useful: he is a cameraman who helped her a great deal when she started to work in television. He is a little older than she, but he has the quality of an eternal worshipful student; he finds her the most beautiful, the most intelligent, and (especially) the most sensitive of all women.

His beloved's sensitivity seems to him like a landscape by a German Romantic painter: scattered with trees in unimaginably contorted shapes, and above them a faraway blue sky, God's dwelling place; each time he steps into this landscape, he feels an irresistible impulse to fall to his knees and to stay fixed there, as if witnessing a divine miracle.

16

The room fills gradually; there are many French entomologists and a few from abroad, among them a Czech in his sixties who people say is some prominent figure in the new regime, a minister perhaps or the president of the Academy of Sciences or at least a member of that academy. In any case, if only from the standpoint of simple curiosity, this is the most interesting figure in the assembly (he represents a new period in history, after Communism has gone off into the mists of time); yet amid this chattering crowd he is standing, tall and awkward, all alone. For a while, people were rushing up to grasp his hand and ask him various questions, but the discussion always ended much sooner than they expected, and after the first four sentences back and forth, they had no idea what to talk to him about next. Because when it came down to it, there was no mutual topic. The French reverted quickly to their own problems, he tried to follow them, from time to time he would remark, "In our country, on the other hand," then, having seen that no one cared what was happening "in our country, on the other hand," he would move off, his face veiled in a melancholy that was neither bitter nor unhappy, but reasonable and almost condescending.

As the others crowd noisily into the lobby with its bar, he enters the empty room where four long tables, arranged in a square, await the start of the conference. By the door is a small table with the list of the participants and a young woman who looks as left behind as he. He leans toward her and tells her his name. She has him pronounce it again, twice. Not daring to ask him a third time, she leafs vaguely through her list for a name that might resemble the sound she has heard.

Full of fatherly goodwill, the Czech scientist leans over the list and finds his name: he puts his finger on it: CECHORIPSKY.

"Ah, Monsieur Sechoripi?" says she.

"It's pronounced 'Tché-kho-rjips-qui.'"

"Oh, that's a tough one!"

"And incidentally, it is not written correctly, either," says the scientist. He takes up the pen he sees on the table, and above the C and the R he draws the little marks that look like inverted circumflexes.

The secretary looks at the marks, looks at the scientist, and sighs: "It's awfully complicated!"

"Not at all, it's very simple."

"Simple?"

"You know Jan Hus?"

The secretary glances quickly over the list of guest conferees, and the Czech scientist hastens to explain: "As you know, he was a great Church reformer in the fourteenth century. A predecessor of Luther. Professor at Charles University, which was the first university to be established in the Holy Roman Empire, as you know. But what you do not know is that Jan Hus was also a great reformer of orthography. He succeeded in making it marvelously simple. In your language, to write what you pronounce 'tch,' you must use three letters, t, c, h. The Germans even need four: t, s, c, h. Whereas, thanks to Jan Hus, all we need in our language is a single letter, c, with that little mark above it."

The scientist leans again over the secretary's table, and in the margin of the list, he writes a c, very big, with an inverted circumflex: Č; then he looks into her eyes and articulates in a very clear, sharp voice: "Tch!"

The secretary looks into his eyes too and repeats: "Tch."

"Yes. Perfect!"

"It's really very useful. Too bad people don't know about Luther's reform anywhere except in your country."

"Jan Hus's reform," says the scientist, acting as if he had not heard the French girl's gaffe, "is not completely unknown. There is one other country where it is used . . . you know where, don't you?"

"No."

"In Lithuania!"

"In Lithuania," the secretary repeats, trying vainly to recall where in the world to place that country.

"And in Latvia too. So now you see why we Czechs are so proud of those little marks over letters. [With a smile:] We would willingly give up anything else. But we will fight for those marks to the last drop of our blood."

He bows to the young woman and moves to the quadrangle of tables. Before each seat is a small card bearing a name. He finds his own, looks at it a long while, takes it up in his fingers and, with a sorrowful but forgiving smile, brings it to show to the secretary.

Meanwhile, another entomologist has stopped at the entrance table to have the young woman circle his name. She sees the Czech scientist and tells him: "Just one moment, Monsieur Chipiqui!"

The Czech makes a magnanimous gesture to indicate: Don't worry, mademoiselle, I'm in no hurry. Patiently, and not without a touching modesty, he waits beside the table (two more entomologists have stopped there), and when the secretary is finally free, he shows her the little place card:

"Look, funny, isn't it?"

She looks without much understanding: "But, Monsieur Chenipiqui, see, the accents, there they are!"

"True, but they are regular circumflexes! They forgot to invert them! And look where they put them! Over the E and the O! Cêchôripsky!"

"Oh yes, you're right!" says the secretary indignantly.

"I wonder," the Czech scientist says with increasing melancholy, "why people always forget them. They are so poetic, these inverted circumflexes! Don't you think so? Like birds in flight! Like doves with wings outspread! [His voice very tender:] Or butterflies, if you prefer."

And he leans again over the table to take up the pen and correct the orthography of his name on the little card. He does it very modestly as if to apologize, and then, without a word, he withdraws.

The secretary watches him go, tall, oddly misshapen, and suddenly feels suffused with maternal fondness. She pictures an inverted circumflex in the form of a butterfly fluttering around the scientist and finally settling on his white mane.

As he moves toward his seat, the Czech scientist turns his head and sees the secretary's tender smile. He responds with his own smile, and along his way he sends her three more. The smiles are melancholy yet proud. A melancholy pride: this would describe the Czech scientist.

17

That he should be melancholy after seeing the circumflexes incorrectly positioned over his name, anyone can understand. But where did he get his pride from?

This is the essential element in his biography: a year after the Russian invasion in 1968, he was driven out of the Entomological Institute and had to become a construction worker, and that went on until the end of the occupation, in 1989, that is, for about twenty years.

But aren't there hundreds, thousands of people losing their jobs all the time in America, in France, in Spain, everywhere? They suffer from it, but they derive no pride from it. Why is the Czech scientist proud and not they?

Because he was driven from his position not for economic reasons but for political ones.

Fine. But in that case, still unexplained is why misfortune from economic causes should be less serious or less noble. Should a man dismissed because he displeased his boss feel shame, whereas one who loses his position over his political views is entitled to boast of it? Why is that?

Because in an economic dismissal the dismissed person plays a passive role: there is no courage in his stance to admire.

This seems an obvious distinction, but it is not.

For the Czech scientist, who was driven from his position after 1968 when the Russian army installed a particularly loathsome regime in the country, had accomplished no act of courage, either. Chief of one of his institute's divisions, he was interested only in flies. One day, with no warning, a dozen notorious opponents of the regime surged into his office and demanded that he give them a room where they could hold semi-clandestine meetings. They were playing by the rules of moral judo: turning up by surprise and making a little audience of observers all by themselves. The unexpected confrontation put the scientist in a complete bind. Saying "yes" would immediately entail disagreeable risks: he could lose his position, and his three children would be barred from the university. But he hadn't enough courage to say "no" to the micro-audience who were already taunting him in advance for cowardice. He therefore ended up agreeing and despised himself for his timidity, his weakness, his incapacity to resist being pushed around. So, to be accurate, it was timorousness, not courage, that eventually got him driven from his position and his children driven from school.

If that is so, then why in hell does he feel proud?

The more time passed, the more he forgot his initial aversion to the opponents and got into the habit of seeing his "yes" back then as a voluntary, free act, the expression of his personal revolt against the hated regime. Thus he has come to count himself among those who stepped onto the great stage of history, and it is from that conviction that he draws his pride.

But isn't it true that countless people are perpetually involved in countless political conflicts and can therefore take pride in having stepped onto the great stage of history?

I should clarify my thesis: the scientist's pride is due to the fact that he stepped onto the stage of history not at just any random moment but at the exact moment when the lights came up on it. The lighted stage of history is termed a Planetary Historic News Event. Prague in 1968, floodlit and observed by cameras, was a Planetary Historic News Event par excellence, and the Czech scientist is proud to feel its kiss upon his brow unto this very day.

But a great trade negotiation, or summit meetings of world powers, these too are important news events, also floodlit, filmed, discussed; how is it they do not arouse in their participants that same thrilled sense of pride?

I hasten to add a final distinction: the Czech scientist was touched not by the grace of just any random Planetary Historic News Event but by the sort termed Sublime. A News Event is Sublime when the man at stage front is suffering while gunfire clatters in the background and the Archangel of Death hovers overhead.

So this is the definitive formulation: the Czech scientist is proud to have been touched by the grace of a Sublime Planetary Historic News Event. He knows full well that this grace sets him apart from all the Norwegians and Danes, all the French and English, present in the room with him.

18

At the head table is a seat where the speakers succeed one another; the Czech scientist is not listening to them. He awaits his own turn, from time to time reaching into his pocket to touch the five sheets of his brief paper, which he knows is no great shakes: having been at a remove from scientific work for twenty years, he could do no more than summarize what he had published when, as a young researcher, he had discovered and described an unknown species of fly which he named *Musca pragensis*. Now, hearing the chairman pronounce the syllables that must surely signify his name, he rises and moves toward the speaker's seat.

In the twenty seconds his journey takes, something unexpected happens to him: he is overcome by emotion: good Lord, after so many years, here he is again among the people he respects and who respect him, among scientists who are kindred minds and from whose midst fate had snatched him; when he stops at the empty chair meant for him, he does not sit; he wants for once to obey his feelings, to be spontaneous and tell his unknown colleagues what he feels.

"Excuse me, my dear ladies and dear gentlemen, for expressing my emotion, which I did not anticipate and which has caught me by surprise. After an absence of twenty years, I am once again able to address a gathering of people who think about the same problems as I do, who are stimulated by the same passion as I am. I come from a country where, merely for saying aloud what he thought, a man could be deprived of the very meaning of his life, since for a man of science the meaning of his life is nothing else but his science. As you know, tens of thousands of men, the entire intelligentsia of my country, were driven from their positions after the tragic summer of 1968. Just six months ago, I was still a construction worker. No, there is nothing humiliating to that, a person learns a lot, earns the friendship of simple, honorable folk, and comes to realize also that we scientific folk are privileged, for to do work that is also our passion is a privilege, yes, my friends, a privilege my fellow construction workers have never known, because it is impossible to be passionate about carrying a girder. This privilege denied me for twenty years I have back now, and I am fairly drunk with it. That, dear friends, is why I see this moment as an enormous celebration, though it remains a somewhat melancholy one."

As he speaks these last words, he feels tears welling in his eyes. That bothers him a little, he sees again the image of his father, who as an old man was continually in an emotional state and wept at every turn, but then he says to himself, why not let go for once: these people should feel honored by his emotion, which he proffers them like a little gift from Prague.

He is not mistaken. The audience too is moved. Hardly has he pronounced the final word than Berck rises and applauds. The camera is there in an instant, it films Berck's face, his hands applauding, and it films the Czech scientist as well. The entire room rises, slowly or swiftly, faces smiling or serious, everyone is clapping, and they enjoy it so much that they do not know when to stop; the Czech scientist stands before them, tall, very tall, awkwardly tall, and the more awkwardness radiates from his figure, the more he is touching and feels touched, so that his tears no longer hide beneath his eyelids but roll solemnly down around his nose, toward his mouth, toward his chin, in full sight of all his colleagues, who start applauding still harder, if possible.

Finally, the ovation thins, people sit back down, and the Czech scientist says in a trembling voice: "I thank you, my friends, I thank you with all my heart." He bows and moves toward his place. And he knows that right now he is living the greatest moment of his life, the moment of glory, yes, of glory, why not say the word, he feels grand and beautiful, he feels famous, and he wants his walk to his seat to be long and never-ending.

19

As he went to his seat, silence reigned in the room. Perhaps it would be more precise to say several silences reigned. The scientist discerned only one: the emotional silence. He did not realize that, gradually, like an imperceptible modulation that moves a sonata from one key to another, the emotional silence had changed into an uneasy silence. Everyone had understood that this gentleman with an unpronounceable name was so moved by himself that he had forgotten to read the paper that was supposed to inform them of his discoveries of new flies. And everyone knew it would have been impolite to remind him of it. After a lengthy hesitation, the conference chairman coughs and says: "I thank Monsieur Tchécochipi . . . [he waits a good moment to give the guest a last chance to remember on his own] . . . and I call on the next speaker." At this point, the silence is briefly broken by a muffled laugh at the far end of the room.

Immersed in his thoughts, the Czech scientist hears neither the laugh nor his colleague's paper. Other speakers follow, until a Belgian scientist, who like him works on flies, awakens him from his meditation: good Lord, he forgot to give his paper! He puts his hand in his pocket, the five sheets are there as proof that he is not dreaming.

His cheeks are burning. He feels ridiculous. Can he still retrieve something of the situation? No, he knows he cannot retrieve anything at all.

After a few moments of shame, a strange idea comes to console him: it's true he is ridiculous; but there is nothing negative, nothing shameful or disagreeable, in that; the ridiculousness that has befallen him intensifies still more the inherent melancholy of his life, renders his destiny still sadder, and hence still grander and more beautiful.

No, pride will never desert the melancholy of the Czech scientist.

20

Every meeting has its deserters who gather in an adjoining room to drink. Vincent, who is weary of listening to the entomologists and was not sufficiently entertained by the Czech scientist's odd performance, turns up in the lobby with the other deserters, around a long table near the bar.

After sitting silent for quite a while, he manages to start a conversation with some strangers: "I have a girlfriend who wants me to get rough."

When it was Pontevin saying that, he paused there for a moment, during which his entire audience fell into an attentive silence. Vincent tries to effect the same pause, and, indeed, he hears laughter, great laughter, rising up: that encourages him, his eyes gleam, he signals with his hand to calm his audience, but just then he registers that they are all looking toward the other end of the table, entertained by the altercation between two gentlemen calling each other names.

After a minute or two, he manages again to make himself heard: "I was in the middle of telling you that my girlfriend keeps wanting me to get rough with her." This time around, everyone is listening to him, and Vincent does not make the mistake of pausing; he talks faster and faster, as if to keep ahead of someone chasing after him to interrupt him: "But I can't do it, I'm too nice, you know?" and in response to these words he himself starts laughing. Seeing that his laughter is unechoed, he hurries to go on and speeds up his delivery still more: "A young typist often comes to my house, I dictate to her. . . ."

"Does she use a computer?" asks a man, suddenly taking an interest.

"Yes," Vincent answers.

"What make?"

Vincent names a make. The man owns a different one, and he starts telling stories about what he has gone through with his computer, which has picked up the habit of playing dirty tricks on him. Everyone is chuckling, and now and then they guffaw.

And Vincent sadly recalls an old idea of his: people always think that a man's fortunes are more or less determined by his appearance, by the beauty or ugliness of his face, by his size, by his hair or lack of it. Wrong. It is the voice that decides it all. And Vincent's is feeble and too piercing; when he starts to talk no one notices, so that he has to force it, and then everyone has the impression he is shouting. Pontevin, by contrast, speaks with utter softness, and his deep voice resounds, pleasing, beautiful, powerful, so that everyone listens only to him.

Ah, that damned Pontevin. He had promised to come with Vincent to the conference and bring the whole gang and then he lost interest, true to his nature, with its tendency toward talk over actions. From one standpoint, Vincent was disappointed, from the other he felt more than ever obliged not to fail the command of his teacher, who on the eve of Vincent's departure had said: "You'll have to represent all of us. I give you full power to act in our name, for our common cause." Of course, it was a joke command, but the gang of cronies at the Café Gascon is convinced that in the senseless world we live in, only joke commands deserve obedience. In his mind's eye, alongside the head of the subtle Pontevin, Vincent could see Machu's enormous mug grinning approval. Fortified by that message and that grin, he decides to take action; he looks around him, and in the group clustered at the bar, he sees a girl he likes.

21

The entomologists are strange boors: they are neglecting the girl even though she is listening to them with the best will in the world, prepared to laugh when she should and to look serious when they indicate. Clearly, she knows none of the men here, and her diligent reactions, which go unnoticed, are cover for a soul struck shy. Vincent gets up from the table, approaches the group the girl is in, and speaks to her. Soon they move apart from the others and grow absorbed in a conversation that proves easy and limitless from the start. Her name is Julie, she is a typist, she did a little job for the chairman of the entomologists; free since the afternoon, she took the opportunity to spend the evening in this famous château among people who intimidate her but who also excite her curiosity, since until yesterday she had never seen an entomologist. Vincent feels comfortable with her, he doesn't need to raise his voice, indeed he lowers it to keep the others from hearing them. Then he draws her over to a little table where they can sit side by side, and he lays his hand over hers.

"You know," he says, "everything depends on the power of the voice. It's more important than having a good-looking face."

"Your voice is lovely."

"You think so?"

"Yes, I do."

"But weak."

"That's what's nice about it. My voice is awful, grating, croaking, like an old crow, don't you think?"

"No," says Vincent with a certain tenderness, "I love your voice, it's provocative, irreverent."

"You think?"

"Your voice is like you!" Vincent says fondly. "You're irreverent and provocative yourself!"

Julie, who loves hearing what Vincent is telling her: "Yes, I think that's so."

"These people are jerks," says Vincent.

She so agrees: "Absolutely."

"Show-offs. Bourgeois. Did you see Berck? What a moron!"

She agrees absolutely. These people behaved to her as if she were invisible, and anything she can hear against them gives her pleasure, she feels avenged. Vincent seems more and more appealing, he's a good-looking fellow, cheerful and unaffected, and he is not a show-off at all.

"I feel," says Vincent, "like raising some real hell here. . . ."

That sounds good: like a promise of mutiny. Julie smiles, she feels like applauding.

"I'm going to get you a whisky!" he tells her, and he sets off to the other end of the lobby, toward the bar.

22

Meanwhile, the chairman closes the conference, the participants noisily leave the room, and the lobby immediately fills up. Berck approaches the Czech scientist. "I was most moved by your . . ." he hesitates purposely, to make clear how hard it is to find a term delicate enough to describe the genre of speech the Czech had made, ". . . by your . . . testimony. We tend to forget too quickly. I'd like to assure you that I have been extremely sensitive to what was happening in your country. You people were the pride of Europe, which hasn't many reasons of its own to be proud."

The Czech scientist makes a vague gesture of protest to indicate his modesty.

"No, don't protest," continues Berck. "I'm determined to say it. You, you especially, the intellectuals of your country, by your determined resistance to Communist oppression, you've shown the courage we often lack, you've shown such a thirst for freedom, I would even say such daring for freedom, that you've become an example to us. Besides," he adds, to give his words a touch of the informal, a sign of partnership, "Budapest is a magnificent, vital city and, allow me to emphasize the point, utterly European."

"You mean Prague?" the Czech scientist asks timidly.

Ah, damn geography! Berck realizes that geography has led him to commit a small error, and mastering his irritation in the face of his colleague's tactlessness, he says: "Of course I mean Prague, but I also mean Cracow, I mean Sofia, I mean Saint Petersburg, I have in mind all those cities of the East that have just emerged from an enormous concentration camp."

"Don't say 'concentration camp.' We often lost our jobs, but we weren't in camps."

"All the countries of the East were covered with camps, my good fellow! Real or symbolic camps, it doesn't matter!"

"And don't say 'the East,'" the Czech scientist goes on with his objections: "Prague, as you know, is as Western a city as Paris. Charles University, which was founded in the fourteenth century, was the first university in the Holy Roman Empire. It was there, as of course you know, that Jan Hus taught, Luther's precursor, the great reformer of the Church and of orthography."

What kind of fly has bitten the Czech scientist? He just doesn't stop correcting his interlocutor, who is enraged by it, although he manages to preserve some warmth in his voice: "My dear colleague, don't be ashamed of coming from the East. France has the warmest feelings for the East. Look at your nineteenth-century emigration!"

"We had no nineteenth-century emigration."

"What about Mickiewicz? I am proud that he

should have found his second homeland in France!"

"But Mickiewicz wasn't . . ." the Czech scientist keeps objecting.

Just then Immaculata arrives on the scene; she makes some vigorous signals to her cameraman and then, with a wave of her hand, moves the Czech to one side, installs herself in front of Berck, and addresses him: "Jacques-Alain Berck . . ."

The cameraman sets the camera back on his shoulder: "Just a minute!"

Immaculata breaks off, looks at the cameraman, and then again at Berck: "Jacques-Alain Berck . . ."

23

When, an hour earlier, Berck saw Immaculata and her cameraman in the conference room, he thought he would howl with fury. But now the irritation caused by the Czech scientist has outstripped the one caused by Immaculata; grateful to her for ridding him of the exotic pedant, he even gives her a vague smile.

Heartened, she takes a cheerful and conspicuously familiar tone: "Jacques-Alain Berck, here in this gathering of entomologists, a family you belong to through the coincidences in your destiny, you've just lived through some emotional moments . . . ," and she thrusts the microphone at his mouth.

Berck answers like a schoolboy: "Yes, we are privileged to welcome here among us a great Czech entomologist who instead of devoting himself to his profession has had to spend his whole life in prison. We were all moved by his presence."

Being a dancer is not only a passion, it is also a road one can never again turn off from; when Duberques humiliated him after the lunch with the AIDS people, Berck went to Somalia not through a surge of vanity but because he felt obliged to make up for a botched dance step. Right now he senses the insipid quality of his remarks, he knows they lack something, a touch of salt, some unexpected idea, a surprise. So, instead of stopping, he goes on talking until he sees, coming toward him from afar, a better

77

inspiration: "And I take this opportunity to announce my proposal to establish a Franco-Czech Entomological Association. [Himself surprised by this idea, he immediately feels much better.] I've just discussed this with my colleague from Prague [he gestures vaguely toward the Czech scientist], who has declared himself delighted with the idea of ornamenting this association with the name of a great exiled poet of the last century who will forever symbolize the friendship between our two peoples. Mickiewicz. Adam Mickiewicz. The life of this poet stands as a lesson that will remind us that everything we do, be it poetry or science, is a revolt. [The word "revolt" puts him definitively back in fine form.] For man is always in revolt [now he's really splendid and he knows it], isn't that so, my friend? [He turns to the Czech scientist, who immediately appears within the camera frame and tilts his head as if to say "yes."] You have proved this by your life, by your sacrifices, by your sufferings, yes, you confirm my belief that any man worthy of the name is always in revolt, in revolt against oppression, and if there is oppression no more . . . [a long pause, Pontevin is the only other person who can do such long and effective pauses; then, in a low voice:] . . . in revolt against the human condition we did not choose."

Revolt against the human condition we did not choose. That last line, the flower of his improvisation, surprises even him; a really beautiful line, actually; it suddenly carries him far beyond the preachings of politicians and puts him in communion with the greatest minds of his land: Camus might have written such a line, Malraux too, or Sartre.

Happy, Immaculata signals the cameraman, and the camera stops.

That's when the Czech scientist approaches Berck and says: "That was very beautiful, really, very beautiful, but permit me to tell you that Mickiewicz was not . . ."

After his public performances, Berck always seems a little drunk; his voice firm, derisive, and loud, he interrupts the Czech scientist: "I know, my dear colleague, I know just as well as you do that Mickiewicz was not an entomologist. In fact, very rarely are poets entomologists. But despite this handicap, they are the pride of the entire human race, of which, if you'll allow me, ento-mologists, yourself included, are a part."

A great liberating laugh bursts out like a head of steam too long confined; indeed, ever since they realized that this gentleman so moved by himself had forgotten to read his paper, the ento-mologists have all been dying to laugh. Berck's impertinent remarks have finally freed them of their scruples, and they roar without bothering to hide their delight.

The Czech scientist is taken aback: what has happened to the respect his colleagues were show-ing him only ten minutes earlier? How is it possi-ble that they are laughing, that they are permitting themselves to laugh? Can people move so easily from veneration to contempt? (Oh yes, dear fellow, oh yes.) Is goodwill so fragile, so precarious a thing, then? (Of course, dear fellow, of course.)

At that same moment Immaculata comes up to Berck. Her voice is loud and sounds tipsy: "Berck, Berck, you're magnificent! It's absolutely you! Oh, I adore your irony! You've certainly used it on me! Remember back in school? Berck, Berck, remember how you used to call me Immaculata? The bird of night that kept you from sleeping! That troubled your dreams! We've got to make a film together, a portrait of you. You really have to agree I'm the only one who has the right to do it."

The laughter the entomologists awarded him for the licking he gave the Czech scientist still echoes in Berck's head, intoxicating him; at moments like this, an enormous self-satisfaction fills him and makes him capable of recklessly frank behavior that often scares even him. So let us forgive him in advance for what he is about to do. He takes Immaculata by the arm, pulls her aside to shield himself from prying ears, and then in a low voice tells her: "Go fuck yourself, you old slut, with your sick neighbors, go fuck yourself, bird of night, night scarecrow, nightmare, reminder of my stupidity, monument of my idiocy, sewage of my memories, stinking piss of my youth . . ."

She listens to him and cannot believe she is really hearing what she is hearing. She thinks he is saying these hideous words for someone else, to cover his tracks, to fool the people around them, she thinks these words are just a trick she doesn't get; so she asks, softly and unaffectedly: "Why are

you saying all this to me? Why? How am I supposed to take it?"

"You're supposed to take it just exactly the
way I'm saying it! Literally! Completely literally! Slut as slut, pain in the ass as pain in the
ass, nightmare as nightmare, piss as piss!"

24

All this time, from the bar in the lobby, Vincent
has been watching the target of his contempt.
The whole scene having taken place some ten
meters away from him, he caught none of the
conversation. One thing, though, seemed clear to
him: Berck looked to him just as Pontevin had
always described him: a mass-media clown, a
ham, a show-off, a dancer. Without a doubt, it
was only because of his presence that a television
crew had deigned to take an interest in the entomologists! Vincent watched him attentively,
studying his art at dancing: the way he never lost
sight of the camera, his skill at always position-
ing himself in front of other people, his elegant

style of making some hand gesture to draw attention to himself. When Berck takes Immaculata
by the arm, he can bear it no longer, and he cries
out: "Look at him, the only thing he cares about
is the woman from the television! He didn't take
his foreign colleague by the arm, he doesn't give
a damn about his colleagues, especially if they're
foreigners, the television is his only master, his
only mistress, his only concubine, because I bet
he hasn't got any others, because I bet he's the
biggest no-balls in the world!"

Oddly, despite its unpleasant weakness, for once
his voice is perfectly audible. Indeed, there is one
circumstance in which even the weakest voice can
be heard. That is when it is putting forth ideas that
irritate us. Vincent goes on to develop his thoughts,
he is witty, he is incisive, he talks about dancers
and the deal they have struck with the Angel, and
increasingly gratified by his eloquence, he climbs
his hyperboles as one climbs the steps of a stairway
to heaven. A young man in eyeglasses, wearing a
three-piece suit, watches and listens to him
patiently, like a predator lying in wait. Then, when
Vincent has exhausted his eloquence, he says:

"Dear sir, we cannot choose the era we are

born into. And we all of us live under the gaze of the cameras. That is part of the human condition from now on. Even when we fight a war, we're fighting it under the eye of the camera. And when we want to protest against anything, we can't make ourselves heard without cameras. We are all dancers, as you say. I would even say: either we're dancers or we're deserters. You seem to regret, dear sir, that time marches on. So go on back! How about to the twelfth century, would you like that? But when you get there you'll start protesting against the cathedrals, as some modern barbarism! So go back further still! Go back to the apes! No modernity to threaten you there, there you'll be completely at home, in the immaculate paradise of the macaques!"

Nothing is more humiliating than not coming up with a slashing retort to a slashing attack. In unspeakable embarrassment, amid jeering laughter, Vincent feebly withdraws. After a minute of consternation, he remembers that Julie is waiting for him; he bolts the drink he has been holding untouched in his hand; then he sets the glass on the bar and picks up two other whiskies, one for himself, the other to take to Julie.

25

The image of the man in the three-piece suit is still stuck like a splinter in his soul, he cannot rid himself of it; this is all the more painful because it comes just when he is hoping to seduce a woman. How can he seduce her if his mind is preoccupied by a painful splinter?

She notices his mood: "Where were you all this time? I thought you weren't coming back. That you were trying to ditch me."

He realizes she cares for him, and that slightly eases the pain from the splinter. He makes a fresh effort to be a charmer, but she is still mistrustful:

"Don't give me any stories. You're different from before. Did you run into someone you know?"

"No, really, no," says Vincent.

"Yes, really, yes. You met a woman. And please, if you want to go off with her, you can do it. Half an hour ago I didn't know you; so I could just go on not knowing you."

She is sadder and sadder, and for a man there is no balm more soothing than the sadness he has caused a woman.

"Really, no, believe me, there's no woman. There was a nuisance, some dismal moron I had an argument with. That's all, that's all," and he strokes her cheek so sincerely, so tenderly, that she drops her suspicions.

"Still, Vincent, you're completely transformed."

"Come," he tells her, and he invites her to go with him to the bar. He wants to extirpate the splinter with a flood of whisky. The elegant fellow in the three-piece suit is still there, with some other people. There's no woman in his vicinity, and that pleases Vincent, accompanied as he is by Julie, whom he finds prettier by the minute. He picks up another two glasses of whisky, gives her one, drinks the other down fast, then leans toward her: "Look over there, that moron in the suit, with the eyeglasses."

"Him? But, Vincent, he's nothing, he's completely nothing, how can you care about him?"

"You're right. He's an underfucked loser. He's an anti-cock. He's a no-balls," says Vincent, and it seems to him that Julie's presence removes him from his defeat, because the real victory, the only one that counts, is the conquest of a woman

86

picked up fast in the grimly unerotic milieu of the entomologists.

"He's nothing, nothing, nothing, I assure you," Julie repeats.

"You're right," says Vincent, "if I keep thinking about him I'll become as moronic as he is," and right there, at the bar, in front of everyone, he kisses her on the mouth.

It is their first kiss.

They go out into the park, stroll, stop, and kiss again. Then they find a bench on the lawn and sit down. From far away the river's murmur reaches them. They are transported, without knowing by what; but I know: they are hearing Madame de T.'s river, the river from her nights of love; from the well of the past, the age of pleasure is sending Vincent a quiet greeting.

And as if he could see it, Vincent says: "In olden times, in these châteaux, there used to be orgies. The eighteenth century, you know. Sade. The Marquis de Sade. *La Philosophie dans le boudoir*. You know that book?"

"No."

"You should read it. I'll lend it to you. It's a

conversation between two men and two women in the middle of an orgy."

"Yes," she says.

"All four of them are naked, making love, all together."

"Yes."

"You'd like that, wouldn't you?"

"I don't know," she says. But that "I don't know" is not a refusal, it is the touching candor of an ideal modesty.

A splinter is not so easily extirpated. It is possible to master the pain, repress it, pretend to forget about it, but that pretense is a strain. Vincent is speaking so passionately of Sade and his orgies less because he hopes to corrupt Julie than because he is trying to forget the insult dealt him by the elegant fellow in the three-piece suit.

"Sure you do," he says, "you know very well you would," and he wraps her in his arms and kisses her. "You know very well you'd like that." And he yearns to quote her dozens of lines, describe scores of situations he knows from that fantastic book called *La Philosophie dans le boudoir*.

Then they rise and continue their stroll. The full moon emerges from the foliage. Vincent looks at Julie and suddenly he is bewitched: the white light has endowed the girl with the beauty of a fairy, a beauty that surprises him, new beauty he did not see in her before, a fine, fragile, chaste, inaccessible beauty. And suddenly, he cannot even tell how it happened, he imagines the hole of her ass. Abruptly, unexpectedly, that image is there, and he will never be rid of it.

Ah, the liberating ass hole! Thanks to it, the elegant fellow in the three-piece suit (at last, at last!) has completely vanished. What several glasses of whisky could not accomplish, an ass hole has achieved in a single second! Vincent winds Julie in his arms, kisses her, strokes her breasts, gazes on her delicate fairylike beauty, and all this time, constantly, he is picturing her ass hole. He has an enormous desire to tell her: "I'm stroking your breasts, but all I'm thinking about is your ass hole." But he cannot do it, the words will not come out of his mouth. The more he thinks about her ass hole, the more Julie is white, diaphanous, and angelic, such that it is impossible for him to pronounce the words aloud.

26

Véra is sleeping, and I, standing at the open window, I am watching two people strolling in the château's park by the light of the moon.

Suddenly I hear Véra's breathing grow rapid, I turn toward her bed and I realize that in another moment she will start to scream. I've never known her to have nightmares! What goes on in this château?

I wake her and she stares at me, her eyes wide, full of fear. Then she speaks pell-mell, as if in a fit of fever: "I was in a very long corridor in this hotel. All of a sudden, from far off, a man appeared and ran toward me. When he got within ten meters, he started to shout. And, imagine, he was speaking Czech! Completely demented things: 'Mickiewicz is not Czech! Mickiewicz is Polish!' Then he came a few steps from me, threatening, and that's when you woke me up."

"Forgive me," I say, "you're the victim of my crazy imagination."

"How do you mean?"

"As if your dreams are a wastebasket where I toss pages that are too stupid."

"What are you inventing? A novel?" she asks, in anguish.

I bow my head.

"You've often told me you wanted to write a novel someday with not a single serious word in it. A Big Piece of Nonsense for Your Own Pleasure. I'm frightened the time may have come. I just want to warn you: be careful."

I bow my head still lower.

"You remember what your mother used to tell you? I can hear her voice as if it were yesterday: 'Milanku, stop making jokes. No one will understand you. You will offend everyone, and everyone will end up hating you.' Remember?"

"Yes," I say.

"I'm warning you. Seriousness kept you safe. The lack of seriousness will leave you naked to the wolves. And you know they're waiting for you, the wolves are."

And after that terrible prophecy, she goes back to sleep.

27

At just about the same time, the Czech scientist has returned to his room, dejected, his soul bruised. His ears are still filled with the laughter that burst forth after Berck's sarcasms. And he is still taken aback: can people really move so easily from veneration to contempt?

And indeed, I wondered, what did become of the kiss that the Sublime Planetary Historic News Event had planted on his brow?

This is where the courtiers of the News Event make their mistake. They do not know that the situations history stages are floodlit only for the first few minutes. No event remains news over its whole duration, merely for a quite brief span of time, at the very beginning. The dying children of Somalia whom millions of spectators used to watch avidly, aren't they dying anymore? What has become of them? Have they grown fatter or thinner? Does Somalia still exist? And in fact did it ever exist? Could it be only the name of a mirage?

The way contemporary history is told is like a

huge concert where they present all of Beethoven's one hundred thirty-eight opuses one after the other, but actually play just the first eight bars of each. If the same concert were given again in ten years, only the first note of each piece would be played, thus one hundred thirty-eight notes for the whole concert, presented as one continuous melody. And in twenty years, the whole of Beethoven's music would be summed up in a single very long buzzing tone, like the endless sound he heard the first day of his deafness.

The Czech scientist is plunged in melancholy, and as a sort of consolation, the idea occurs to him that from the period of his heroic labor in construction, which everyone wants to forget, he still retains a material and palpable souvenir: an excellent physique. A discreet smile of satisfaction plays over his face, for he is certain that among the people here, no one has muscles like his.

Yes, believe it or not, this seemingly laughable idea really does him good. He throws off his jacket and stretches out flat on his stomach on the floor. Then he raises himself on his arms. He repeats this movement twenty-six times, and he is proud of himself. He remembers when he and his mates would go swimming after work in a little pond behind the construction site. To tell the truth, he was a hundred times happier then than he is today in this château. The workmen used to call him Einstein, and they were fond of him.

And the idea occurs to him, a frivolous idea (he recognizes the frivolity and is even pleased by it), to go for a swim in the fine hotel pool. With a joyous and fully conscious vanity, he means to show off his body to the feeble intellectuals of this sophisticated, overcultivated, and ultimately perfidious country. Fortunately, he has brought his bathing trunks along from Prague (he takes them with him everywhere); he puts them on and looks at himself, half naked, in the mirror. He flexes his arms, and his biceps swell magnificently. "If anyone tried to deny my past, here are my muscles, irrefutable proof!" He imagines his body parading around the pool, showing the French that there exists one utterly fundamental value, bodily perfection, the perfection he personally can boast and that none of them has any idea of. Then he decides it's a little unseemly to walk nearly naked through the hotel corridors, and he pulls on an undershirt. Now for the feet.

Leaving them bare seems to him as inappropriate as putting on shoes; so he decides to wear only socks. Thus clothed, he looks one more time in the mirror. Again his melancholy is joined by pride, and again he feels sure of himself.

28

Ass hole. It could be said otherwise, for instance, as Guillaume Apollinaire did: the ninth portal of your body. His poem on the nine portals of a woman's body exists in two versions: the first he sent to his mistress Lou in a letter written from the trenches on May 11, 1915, and the other he sent from the same place to another mistress, Madeleine, on September 21 of the same year. The poems, both beautiful, differ in their imagery but are constructed in the same fashion: each stanza is devoted to one portal of the beloved's body: one eye, the other eye, the right nostril, the left nostril, the mouth; then, in the poem for Lou, "the portal of your rump" and, finally, the ninth portal, the vulva. But in the second poem, the one for Madeleine, there occurs at the end a curious switch of portals. The vulva recedes to eighth place, and it is the ass hole, opening "between two pearly mountains," that becomes the ninth portal: "yet more mysterious than the others," the portal "of the sorceries one dares not speak of," the "supreme portal."

I consider those four months and ten days between the two poems, four months Apollinaire spent in the trenches, deep in intense erotic reveries that brought him to that shift in perspective, to that revelation: the ass hole is the miraculous focal point for all the nuclear energy of nakedness. The vulva portal is important, of course (of course, who would deny that?), but too officially important, a registered site, classified, documented, explicated, examined, experimented on, watched, sung, celebrated. Vulva: noisy crossroads where all of chattering humankind meets, a tunnel the generations file through. Only the gullible believe in the intimacy of that site, the most public site of all. The only site that is truly intimate, whose taboo even pornographic films respect, is the hole of the ass, the supreme portal; supreme because it is the most mysterious, the most secret.

This wisdom, which cost Apollinaire four months spent beneath a firmament of artillery shells, Vincent attained in the course of a single stroll with Julie, turned diaphanous by the light of the moon.

29

A difficult situation when all you can talk about is one thing and you're not in a position to talk about it: the unuttered ass hole is stuck in Vincent's mouth like a gag. He looks to heaven as if he hopes to find some help there. And heaven grants him what he needs: it sends him poetic inspiration; Vincent exclaims: "Look!" and points to the moon. "It looks like an ass hole drilled into the sky!"

He turns his gaze on Julie. Transparent and tender, she smiles and says "Yes," because for an hour already she has been disposed to admire any remark that comes from him.

He hears her "yes" and still hungers for more. She has the chaste look of a fairy, and he would like to hear her say "ass hole." He wants to see her fairy mouth articulate that word, oh how he wants that! He would like to tell her: "Say it with me: ass hole, ass hole, ass hole," but he does not dare. Instead, ensnared by his own eloquence, he gets more and more tangled up in his metaphor: "The ass hole giving off a lurid light that floods the guts of the universe!" And he stretches an arm to the moon: "Onward, into the ass hole of infinity!"

I cannot help making a small comment on Vincent's improvisation: by his acknowledged obsession with the ass hole, he believes he is enacting his fondness for the eighteenth century, for Sade and the whole gang of libertines; but as if he hadn't the strength to pursue that obsession fully and to the furthest limit, another legacy—a very different, even contrary one, from the following century—hastens to his aid; in other words, he is incapable of discussing his fine libertine obsessions except by making them lyrical; by turning them into metaphors. Thus he sacrifices the spirit of libertinage to the spirit of poetry. And he transfers the ass hole from a woman's body up to the sky.

Ah, this displacement is regrettable, painful to see! I dislike following Vincent along that path:

he struggles, stuck in his metaphor like a fly in glue; he cries out: "The ass hole of the sky like the eye of God's camera!"

As if she sees them winding down, Julie breaks into Vincent's poetic gyrations by pointing to the lighted lobby inside the great windows: "Almost everyone's already left."

They go indoors: it's true, only a few people are still lingering at the tables. The elegant fellow in the three-piece suit is gone. However, his absence recalls him to Vincent so powerfully that he hears that voice again, cold and spiteful, backed by his colleagues' laughter. Again he feels shame: how could he have been so rattled by the fellow? so miserably mute? He strains to clear him from his mind, but he can't do it, he rehears the fellow's words: "We all of us live under the gaze of the cameras. That is part of the human condition from now on. . . ."

He completely forgets about Julie, and, in amazement, he fixes on those two lines; how bizarre: the elegant fellow's argument is almost identical to the objection Vincent himself had raised earlier with Pontevin: "If you want to step into some public dispute, call attention to some

99

horror, how can you do it nowadays without being, or looking like, a dancer?"

Is that the reason he was so disconcerted by the elegant fellow? Was the man's thinking too close to Vincent's own for him to attack it? Are we all of us in the same trap, taken aback by a world that has suddenly changed under our feet into a stage set with no way out? Is there really no difference, then, between what Vincent thinks and what the elegant fellow thinks?

No, that idea is unbearable! He scorns Berck, he scorns the elegant fellow, and his scorn precedes his every judgment. Stubborn, he strains to grasp the difference that separates him from them, until he manages to see it with total clarity: like miserable flunkies, they delight in the human condition just as it is imposed on them: dancers happy to be dancers. Whereas he, even though he knows there is no way out, proclaims his disagreement with that world. Then he thinks of the answer he should have thrown in the elegant fellow's face: "If living under cameras has become our condition, I revolt against it. I did not choose it!" That's the answer! He leans toward Julie and without a word of explanation tells her: "The only thing left for us is to revolt against the human condition we did not choose!"

Already accustomed to Vincent's oddly timed remarks, she finds this one splendid and responds in a pugnacious tone herself: "Absolutely!" And as if the word "revolt" had filled her with a giddy energy, she says: "Let's go up to your room, the two of us."

At once, again, the elegant fellow has vanished from Vincent's head as he looks at Julie, marveling at her latest words.

She is marveling too. Near the bar there are still a few of the people she had been standing with before Vincent spoke to her. Those people had acted as if she did not exist. She had been humiliated. Now she looks at them, regal, untouchable. They no longer impress her. She has a night of love ahead of her, and she has it through her own will, through her own courage; she feels rich, lucky, and stronger than any of those people.

She breathes into Vincent's ear: "They're all a bunch of anti-cocks." She knows that's Vincent's word, and she says it to show she is giving herself to him and belongs to him.

It is as if she had put a grenade of euphoria into

his hand. He could go now with the beautiful bearer of the ass hole, right into his room, but, as if he were following a command issued from a distance, he feels obliged to raise some hell here before he goes. He is caught up in a drunken whirlpool where the image of the ass hole merges with the imminence of sex, the elegant fellow's jeering voice, and the silhouette of Pontevin, who, like some Trotsky, is running a huge uprising, a great riotous mutiny, from his Paris bunker.

"We're going to have a swim," he announces to Julie, and he runs down the staircase to the pool, which at the moment is empty and has the look of a theater stage to the people up above. He unbuttons his shirt. Julie runs to join him. "We're going to have a swim," he repeats, and tosses his trousers aside. "Take off your clothes!"

30

The dreadful speech Berck directed at Immaculata was uttered in a low, hissing voice, so the people nearby could not grasp the real nature of the drama playing out before their eyes. Immaculata managed to let nothing show; when Berck turned away, she moved to the staircase, climbed it, and only when she was finally alone, in the deserted corridor leading to the rooms, did she realize she was staggering.

Half an hour later, the unsuspecting cameraman came into the room they shared and found her on the bed, lying flat on her stomach.

"What's wrong?"

She does not answer.

He sits down beside her and lays his hand on her head. She shakes it off as if a snake had touched her.

"But what's wrong?"

He repeats the same question several times more, until she says: "Please go gargle, I can't stand bad breath."

He did not have bad breath, he was always well scrubbed and scrupulously clean, therefore he knew she was lying, yet he goes docilely into the bathroom to do as she ordered.

The bad-breath idea did not occur to Immaculata out of nowhere, for what inspired that mischief was a recent memory immediately repressed: the memory of Berck's bad breath. While she was listening, crushed, to his insults, she was in no state to concern herself with his exhalation, and it was an observer hidden inside her who registered the nauseating odor and added this clear-mindedly concrete commentary besides: A man whose mouth stinks has no mistress; no woman would put up with it; any woman would find a way to let him know he stinks and would force him to rid himself of that fault. While she was being bombarded with insults, she was listening to this silent commentary, which she found happy and hopeful, because it told her that, despite the specter of gorgeous women Berck cannily allows to hover around him, he has long since lost interest in romantic adventures, and that the place beside him in bed is vacant.

As he gargles, the cameraman, a man at once romantic and practical, says to himself that the only way to change his companion's foul mood is to make love to her as soon as possible. So in the bathroom he puts on his pajamas, and, his step tentative, he returns to sit beside her on the edge of the bed.

Not daring to touch her, he asks again: "What's wrong?"

With implacable presence of mind, she responds: "If you can't say anything but that idiotic line, I guess there's not much to gain from a conversation with you."

She rises and goes to the closet; she opens it to consider the few dresses she has hung there; the dresses appeal to her; they rouse a vague but strong wish to not let herself be driven from the scene; to pass again through the precincts of her humiliation; to not consent to her defeat; and if defeat there is, to transform it into great theater, in the course of which she will set her wounded beauty shining and deploy her rebellious pride.

"What are you doing? Where are you going?" he says.

"It doesn't matter. All that matters is not to stay with you."

"But tell me what's wrong!"

Immaculata gazes at her dresses and remarks: "Sixth time," and I would point out that she is not mistaken in her count.

"You were perfect," says the cameraman, determined to ignore her mood. "We were right to come.

Your Berck project looks like a sure thing to me. I ordered up a bottle of champagne to our room."

"You can drink what you want with whoever you want."

"But what's wrong?"

"Seventh time. It's finished with you. For good. I've had enough of the smell that comes out of your mouth. You're my nightmare. My bad dream. My failure. My shame. My humiliation. My disgust. I have to tell you this. Brutally. No more dragging out my hesitation. No more dragging out my nightmare. No more dragging out this business that's stopped making any sense."

She is standing with her face to the open closet, her back to the cameraman, she is speaking calmly, with composure, her voice low, hissing. Then she begins to undress.

31

This is the first time she has undressed before him with such absence of modesty, with such pointed disregard. This undressing signifies: your

106

presence here before me has no, absolutely no, importance; your presence is equivalent to that of a dog or a mouse. Your gaze will not stir a single cell of my body. I could do anything at all in front of you, the most offensive acts, I could vomit in front of you, wash my ears or my crotch, masturbate, piss. You are a non-eye, a non-ear, a non-head. My proud disregard is a cloak that lets me move about before you with complete freedom and complete immodesty.

The cameraman sees his mistress's body change utterly before his eyes: this body which hitherto would give itself to him promptly and simply now rises up in front of him like a Greek statue set on a pedestal a hundred meters high. He is mad with desire, and it is a strange desire, which does not express itself sensually but fills his head and only his head, desire as cerebral fascination, as idée fixe, mystical madness, the certainty that this body, and no other, is the one fated to fulfill his life, his entire life.

She feels that fascination, that devotion, adhere to her skin, and a wave of cold rises to her head. She is surprised at this herself, she has never experienced this sort of wave. It is a wave of cold as there are waves of passion, of heat, or of anger. For that cold really is a passion; as if the cameraman's absolute devotion and Berck's absolute rejection were two faces of the same curse she is fighting off; as if Berck's rebuff were intended to thrust her back into the arms of her commonplace lover and the only way to parry the rebuff were absolute hatred of that lover. This is why she is rejecting him so furiously and wants to turn him into a mouse, that mouse into a spider, and that spider into a fly devoured by another spider.

She is already dressed again, in a white dress, determined to go downstairs and display herself to Berck and all the others. She is pleased to have brought a dress that is white, the color of marriage, for she feels as if this is the day of a wedding, a reverse wedding, a tragic wedding without a groom. Beneath her white dress she bears the wound of an injustice, and she feels she is made greater by that injustice, made more beautiful by it as characters in tragedies are made more beautiful by their suffering. She approaches the door, knowing that the man, in his pajamas, will follow on her heels and will stick behind her like an adoring dog, and she wants them to go through the château like that, a tragi-grotesque couple, a queen with a mutt following behind her.

32

But the man she has relegated to canine status surprises her. He is standing in the doorway and his face is furious. His will to submit has suddenly run out. He is filled with the desperate desire to stand up to this beauty who is humiliating him unjustly. He cannot muster the courage to slap her, beat her, throw her onto the bed and rape her, but he feels all the greater need to do something irreparable, something immensely vulgar and aggressive.

She is forced to stop at the door. "Let me by."

"I won't let you by," he tells her.

"You no longer exist for me."

"What do you mean, I no longer exist?"

"I don't know you."

He laughs tensely: "You don't know me?" He

raises his voice: "We fucked just this morning!"

"I forbid you to talk to me that way! Not with those words!"

"Just this morning you said those words to me yourself, you said, 'Fuck me, fuck me, fuck me!'"

"That was when I still loved you," she said, slightly uncomfortable, "but now those words are nothing but obscenities."

He shouts: "We did fuck, though!"

"I forbid you!"

"And last night we fucked, we fucked, we fucked!"

"Stop it!"

"How come you can stand my body in the morning and not in the evening?"

"You know I detest vulgarity!"

"I don't give a damn what you detest! You're a slut!"

Ah, he should not have used that word, the same one Berck had flung at her. She shouts: "Vulgarity disgusts me and you disgust me!"

He shouts too: "So you fucked a person who disgusts you! But a woman who fucks someone who disgusts her is exactly that, a slut, a slut, a slut!"

The cameraman's talk is coarser by the minute, and fear grows on Immaculata's face.

Fear? Is she really afraid of him? I don't believe that: she knows quite well, in her inmost heart, that it doesn't do to exaggerate the significance of this rebellion. She knows the cameraman's submissiveness and is still confident of it. She knows he is insulting her because he wants to be heard, seen, considered. He is insulting her because he is weak and because all he has in the way of strength is his coarseness, his aggressive talk. If she loved him, even just a tiny bit, she would have to be touched by that explosion of desperate powerlessness. But instead of being touched, she feels an uncontrollable drive to hurt him. And for that very reason she decides to treat his words literally, to believe his insults, to fear them. And that is why she stares at him with eyes that mean to look frightened.

He sees fear in Immaculata's face and feels encouraged: he is usually the one who's frightened, who gives way, who apologizes, and suddenly, because he showed his strength, his rage, it's she who is trembling. Thinking that she is acknowledging her weakness, capitulating, he

111

raises his voice and continues to spout his aggressive and impotent cretinisms. Poor fellow, he does not know that it's still her game he is playing, that he is still a manipulated thing even at the moment he believes he has found power and freedom in his anger.

She tells him: "You scare me. You're odious, you're violent," and he, poor fellow, does not know this is an indictment that will never be quashed and that he, this little scrap of goodness and submissiveness, will thus become now and forever a rapist and an aggressor.

"You scare me," she says again, and she moves him aside so she can leave the room.

He lets her pass and follows her like a mutt following behind a queen.

33

Nudity. I still have a clipping from an October 1993 *Nouvel Observateur*, an opinion poll: twelve hundred people describing themselves as on the left were sent a list of two hundred ten words and asked to underline the ones that fascinated them, that appealed to them, that they found attractive and congenial; a few years earlier, the same poll had been taken: back then, of the same two hundred ten words there were eighteen on which left-wingers agreed and which thereby confirmed the existence of a shared sensibility. In 1993, the beloved words were down to three. Only three words that the left can agree on? What a decline! What a collapse! And what three words are they? Listen to this: "revolt"; "red"; "nudity." "Revolt" and "red," those are obvious. But that, aside from those two words, only "nudity" quickens the heart of left-wingers, that only nudity still stands as their shared symbolic legacy, is astounding. Is this our total inheritance from the magnificent two-hundred-year history solemnly launched by the French Revolution, is this the legacy of Robespierre, Danton, Jaurès, Rosa Luxemburg, of Lenin, Gramsci, Aragon, Che Guevara? Nudity? The naked belly, naked balls, naked buttocks? Is that the last flag under which the final brigades of the left simulate their grand march through the centuries?

But why nudity, exactly? What is the meaning

113

for people on the left of this word they under-lined in the list sent them by a polling agency?

I recall the procession of German leftists in the seventies who were registering their anger against something or other (a nuclear power station, a war, the power of money, I don't remember what) by taking off their clothes and marching, naked and howling, through the streets of a big German city.

What was their nudity supposed to express?

First Hypothesis: To them it represented the most cherished of all freedoms, the value most in danger. The German leftists crossed the city showing their naked genitals the way persecuted Christians went to their deaths carrying a wooden cross on their shoulders.

Second Hypothesis: The German leftists were seeking not to display the symbol of a particular value, but simply to shock a detested audience. Shock it, frighten it, infuriate it. Bombard it with elephant dung. Dump the sewage of the universe on it.

A curious dilemma: does nudity symbolize the greatest of all values, or the greatest filth to be pitched like an excrement bomb onto a crowd of enemies?

And then what does it mean for Vincent when he tells Julie again: "Take off your clothes," and adds: "A huge happening right under the eyes of those underfucked losers!"

And what does it mean for Julie, who, compliant and even rather enthusiastic, says: "Why not?" and unbuttons her dress.

34

He is naked. He's a little astonished at the fact, and laughs a throat-clearing laugh directed more to himself than to her, because being naked like this in this huge glassed-in space is so unaccustomed for him that all he can think of is the weirdness of the situation. She has already thrown off her brassiere, then her underpants, but Vincent is not really seeing her: he registers that she is naked but without knowing what she is like, naked. Let's remember, only a few minutes earlier he was obsessed by the image of her ass hole; is he still thinking about it now that the hole is freed from the silk of her underpants? No.

The ass hole has evaporated from his head. Instead of attentively considering the body that bared itself in his presence, instead of drawing near to it, of slowly apprehending it, perhaps touching it, he turns away and dives.

An odd youngster, this Vincent. He rails against dancers, he raves on about the moon, and underneath it all he is a jock. He dives into the water and swims. He immediately forgets about his own nakedness, forgets about Julie's, and thinks of nothing but his crawl. Behind him, Julie, who doesn't know how to dive, makes her way cautiously down the ladder. And Vincent does not even turn his head to look at her! That's his loss: for she is lovely, very lovely, Julie. Her body seems to glow; not from her modesty, but from something just as fine: from the awkward-ness that comes of solitary privacy, for as Vincent has his head underwater, she is confident that no one is looking at her; the water reaches to her pubic thatch and feels cold; she would love to get all the way in but she hasn't the nerve. She stops and lingers; then, cautiously, she steps down another rung so that the water rises to her navel; she dips her hand and, caressing, she cools her breasts. It is truly beautiful to watch her. The simplehearted Vincent has no idea, but what I myself see here, at last, is a nudity that represents nothing at all, neither freedom nor filth, a nudity divested of all meaning, nudity denuded, just that, pure, and bewitching to a man.

Finally, she starts to swim. She swims much more slowly than Vincent, her head lifted clumsily above the water; Vincent has already done three fifteen-meter laps when she heads for the ladder to climb out. He hurries after her. They are up on the edge when they hear voices from above.

Spurred by the proximity of invisible strangers, Vincent starts shouting: "I'm going to bugger you!" and grinning like a satyr, he lunges at her.

How is it that in the privacy of their stroll together he never dared breathe a single little obscenity to her, but now, when he risks being heard by all kinds of people, he's yelling outrageous things?

Precisely because he has imperceptibly left the zone of intimacy. A word uttered in a small enclosed space has a different meaning from the same word resonating in an amphitheater. No longer is it a word for which he holds full responsibility and which is addressed exclusively to the partner, it is a word that other people demand to hear, people who are there, looking at them. True, the amphitheater is empty, but even though it is empty, the audience, imagined and imaginary, potential and virtual, is there, is with them.

We might wonder who makes up this audience; I do not believe that Vincent pictures the people he saw at the conference; the audience around him now is sizable, insistent, demanding, agitated, curious, but also completely unidentifiable, their features blurred; does this mean that the audience he imagines is the same one dancers dream of? the invisible audience? the one Pontevin is building his theories on? the entire world? an infinitude without faces? an abstraction? Not completely: for behind that anonymous welter a few identifiable faces show through: Pontevin and some other cronies; they are watching the whole scene with some amusement, they are watching Vincent, Julie, and even the audience of strangers surrounding them. It is for them that Vincent is shouting his words, it is their admiration, their approval, he hopes to win.

"You're not going to bugger me!" cries Julie,

who knows nothing of Pontevin but who, she too, is uttering that line for those who are not there but could be there. Does she desire their admiration? Yes, but she desires it only to please Vincent. She wants to be applauded by an unknown and invisible audience in order to be loved by the man she has chosen for this night and—who knows?—for many more. She goes running around the swimming pool and her two breasts swing merrily to right and left.

Vincent's words are bolder and bolder; only their metaphoric nature casts a light mist over their robust vulgarity.

"I'll stick my cock through you and nail you to the wall!"

"You won't nail me anywhere!"

"You'll hang there crucified on the pool ceiling!"

"I won't hang there crucified!"

"I'll tear open your ass hole for the whole world to see!"

"You won't tear it open!"

"Everybody will see your ass hole!"

"Nobody will see my ass hole!" cries Julie.

Just then, again, they hear voices, whose proximity seems to weigh down Julie's light step, to hint that she should stop: she begins to scream in a strident voice like a woman who is just about to be raped. Vincent snatches her and falls with her onto the floor. Her eyes wide, she looks at him, awaiting a penetration she has decided not to resist. She spreads her legs. Closes her eyes. Turns her head slightly to one side.

35

The penetration did not take place. It did not take place because Vincent's member is as small as a wilted wild strawberry, as a great-grand-mother's thimble.

Why is it so small?

I put that question directly to Vincent's member and frankly, astonished, it replies: "And why shouldn't I be small? I saw no need to get big! Believe me, the idea really didn't occur to me! I was not alerted. Vincent and I both watched that odd run of hers around the pool, I was eager to see what would happen next! It was a lot of fun! Now you're going to accuse Vincent of impo-

tence! Excuse me! That would lay a terrific bur-
den of guilt on me, and it would be unfair,
because we live in perfect harmony, he and I, and
I swear to you, we've never let each other down!
I've always been proud of him and he of me!"

The member was telling the truth. And in fact,
Vincent was not unduly vexed by its behavior. If
his member acted that way in the privacy of his
apartment, he would never forgive it. But in
these circumstances, he is inclined to consider its
reaction reasonable and even rather proper. He
therefore decides to take matters as they are and
sets about simulating coition.

Nor is Julie vexed or frustrated. Feeling
Vincent's movements on her body and feeling
nothing inside her she finds strange but, all
things considered, acceptable, and she responds
to her lover's thuds with movements of her own.

The voices they heard have moved away, but a
new sound echoes in the resonant space of the
pool area: the footfalls of a runner passing very
near them.

Vincent's panting gets faster and louder; he
moans and bellows, while Julie emits whimpers
and sobs, partly because Vincent's wet body is

hurting her as it lands on her again and again, and partly because it is her way of answering his roars.

36

Having spotted them only at the last moment, the Czech scientist could not avoid them. But he acts as if they are not there and tries to set his gaze elsewhere. He is nervous: he is not yet familiar with life in the West. In the Communist empire, making love on the edge of a swimming pool was impossible, like, for that matter, many other things he would now have to learn patiently. He has already reached the other side of the pool, and he gets an impulse to turn around and take at least a quick look at the copulating couple; because there's one thing nagging at him: that man copulating, is his body in good shape? Which is more effective for bodybuilding, lovemaking or manual labor? But he restrains himself, since he does not want to be taken for a voyeur.

He stops on the opposite edge and starts to do

exercises: first he runs in place, lifting his knees very high; then he stands on his hands, with his feet in the air; as a child he learned to master that gymnastic position called the handstand, and he does it as well today as he did back then; a question occurs to him: how many great French scientists can do it the way he does? and how many cabinet ministers? He pictures in sequence all the French ministers he knows by name and by photo, he tries to picture them in this position, balanced on their hands, and he is satisfied: as he sees them, they're clumsy and weak. Having accomplished seven handstands, he lies down flat on his stomach and raises himself on his arms.

37

Neither Julie nor Vincent bothers with what is going on around them. They are not exhibitionists, they do not seek to arouse themselves by other people's gaze, to attract that gaze, to watch the person watching them; this is not an orgy they're conducting, it is a show, and during a performance actors try not to meet the audience's eyes. Even more than Vincent, Julie is determined to see nothing; however, the gaze that has just come to rest on her face is too heavy for her not to feel it.

She raises her eyes and sees her: the woman is wearing a gorgeous white dress and is staring at her fixedly; her gaze is strange, remote, and yet heavy, terribly heavy; heavy like despair, heavy like I-don't-know-what-to-do, and beneath this weight, Julie feels almost paralyzed. Her movements slow, falter, cease; a few more whimpers and she is silent.

The woman in white is battling an enormous urge to howl. She cannot free herself of that urge, which is all the stronger for the fact that the man she wants to howl for will not hear her. Suddenly, no longer able to hold on, she emits a cry, a shrill, terrible cry.

Julie thereupon wakes from her stupor, stands, picks up her underpants, puts them on, rapidly covers herself with her disordered clothes, and takes off at a run.

Vincent is slower. He collects his shirt, his trousers, but cannot see his undershorts anywhere.

A few steps back, a man in pajamas stands stock-still; no one sees him nor does he see anyone else, focused as he is on the woman in white.

38

Unable to resign herself to the idea that Berck has rejected her, she had this insane idea to go provoke him, to parade before him in all her white beauty (wouldn't an immaculate's beauty be white?), but her passage through the corridors and lobbies of the château went badly: Berck was gone, and the cameraman followed her not silently, like a humble mutt, but talking at her in a loud, unpleasant voice. She succeeded in drawing attention, but a nasty, sneering attention, so she quickened her pace; thus, in flight, she reached the edge of the pool, where she ran into a couple copulating and emitted her cry.

That cry has roused her: now she suddenly sees with utter clarity the snare closing around her: her pursuer behind, the water ahead. She understands clearly that this encirclement affords no way out; that the only way out available to her is a crazy way out; that the only reasonable action left for her is an insane action; so with the full power of her will she chooses madness: she takes two steps forward and leaps into the water.

The way she has leapt is rather curious: unlike Julie, she knows very well how to dive; and yet she has gone into the water feetfirst, her arms stuck out gracelessly.

Because beyond their practical function, all gestures have a meaning that exceeds the intention of those who make them; when people in bathing suits fling themselves into the water, it is joy itself that shows in the gesture, notwithstanding any sadness the divers may actually feel. When someone jumps into the water fully clothed, it is another thing entirely: the only person who jumps into the water fully clothed is a person trying to drown; and a person trying to drown does not dive headfirst; he lets himself fall: thus speaks the immemorial language of gestures. That is why, though an excellent swimmer, Immaculata in her beautiful dress could only jump into the water in a hideous way.

For no reasonable reason she now finds herself

126

in the water; she is there under the rule of her gesture, whose meaning is little by little filling her soul; she senses that she is living out her suicide, her drowning, and anything she does from now on will only be a ballet, a pantomime through which her tragic gesture will extend its unspoken statement:

After her fall into the water, she stands upright. The pool is not very deep at that spot, the water reaches to her waist; she stays thus for a few moments, her head high, her torso arched. Then she lets herself fall again. A scarf from her dress works free and floats behind her the way memories float behind the dead. Again she stands up, her head tipped back slightly, her arms spread; as if to run, she moves forward a few steps, where the pool floor slants down, then she goes under again. Thus she proceeds, like some aquatic animal, a mythological duck letting its head vanish beneath the surface and then raising it, tipping it upward. These movements sing the yearning to live in the heights or else perish in the watery deep.

The man in pajamas drops suddenly to his knees and sobs: "Come back, come back, I'm a criminal, I'm a criminal, come back!"

39

From the other end of the pool, over where the water is deep, the Czech scientist doing push-ups watches in total astonishment: at first he thought the newly arrived couple had come to join the copulating couple and that he was finally going to see one of those legendary orgies he used to hear so much about when he was working on the scaffoldings of the puritan Communist empire. Out of delicacy, he even thought that in such circumstances of collective coition he ought to quit the pool area and go to his room. Then that cry stabbed his ears, and, his arms braced, he stayed that way as if petrified, unable to go on with his exercises even though he had done only eighteen push-ups. Before his eyes, the woman in the white dress fell into the water, and a scarf began floating behind her, along with a few tiny artificial flowers, blue and pink.

Immobile, his torso raised, the Czech scientist eventually understands that this woman is bent on drowning: she is trying to hold her head underwater but her will is not strong enough, and she keeps coming upright again. He is witnessing a suicide such as he could never have imagined. The woman is sick or wounded or hunted down, again and again she stands upright and vanishes beneath the surface, she must surely not know how to swim; as she proceeds along the pool's incline she ducks deeper each time, so that soon the water will cover her completely and she will die beneath the passive gaze of a man in pajamas kneeling at the edge of the pool, who is watching her and weeping.

The Czech scientist can hesitate no longer: he rises, bends forward over the water, legs flexed, arms stretched behind him.

The man in pajamas no longer sees the woman, fascinated as he is by the figure of an unknown man—tall, strong, strangely misshapen—directly across from him, some fifteen meters away, who is preparing to intervene in a drama that has nothing to do with him, a drama that the man in pajamas reserves jealously to himself and the woman he loves. For there's no doubt about it, he does love her, his hatred was only transitory; he is incapable of detesting her truly and lastingly even if she does make him suffer. He knows she is act-

129

ing under the *diktat* of her irrational, ungovern-
able sensitivity, that miraculous sensitivity of hers
which he cannot comprehend and which he
reveres. Even though he has just heaped abuse on
her, in his heart he is convinced that she is innocent and that someone else is really to blame for
their unexpected discord. He doesn't know who it
is, doesn't know where to find him, but he is set
to tear him apart. In that state of mind, he looks
at the man leaning athletically out over the water;
as if hypnotized, he looks at the man's body,
strong, thick-muscled, and oddly ill-propor-
tioned, with broad womanish thighs and heavy
unintelligent calves, a body as absurd as injustice
incarnate. He knows nothing about this man, has
no reason to mistrust him, but, blinded by his
suffering, he sees in this monument of ugliness
the image of his own inexplicable misery and is
gripped by an invincible hatred for the man.

The Czech scientist dives and, in a few powerful strokes, draws close to the woman.

"Leave her alone!" shouts the man in pajamas, and he too jumps into the water.

The scientist is only two meters away from the
woman; his feet are already touching bottom.

The man in pajamas is swimming toward him and yelling again: "Leave her alone! Don't touch her!"

The Czech scientist stretches an arm beneath the body of the woman as she crumples with a long sigh.

The man in pajamas has got to them now: "Drop her or I kill you!"

Through his tears, he sees nothing before him, nothing but a misshapen silhouette. He grabs it by one shoulder and shakes it violently. The scientist capsizes, the woman falls from his arms. Neither man gives her another thought; she swims to the ladder and climbs up it. The scientist looks at the hate-filled eyes of the man in pajamas, and his own eyes flare with the same hatred.

The man in pajamas holds back no more, and he strikes.

The scientist feels a pain in the mouth. With his tongue he explores a front tooth and discovers that it is loose. This is a false tooth very laboriously screwed into the root by a Prague dentist who had fitted other false teeth around it; the dentist had explained emphatically that this tooth would be serving as a support to the others and that if he should someday lose it, he would be doomed to a denture, a thing the Czech scientist regards with unspeakable horror. His tongue probes the loose tooth and he turns pale, first from anguish and then from rage. His whole life rises before him, and for the second time that day, tears flood his eyes; yes, he is weeping, and from the depth of those tears an idea rises to his head: he has lost everything, all he has left is his muscles; but those muscles, those wretched muscles, what good do they do him? Like a spring, the question sets his right arm into terrible motion: from it comes a punch, a punch as huge as the sorrow of a denture, huge as a half century of wild fucking at the edges of all the swimming pools of France. The man in pajamas vanishes beneath the water.

His collapse is so swift, so thorough, that the Czech scientist thinks he has killed him; after a moment of stupefaction, he bends, lifts him up, gives him a few light taps on the face; the man opens his eyes, his vacant gaze falls on the misshapen apparition, then he frees himself and swims toward the ladder to rejoin the woman.

40

Crouched on the edge of the pool, she has been attentively watching the man in pajamas, his battle and his collapse. Once he has climbed onto the tiled edge of the pool, she stands up and walks toward the staircase, without looking back but slowly enough for him to follow. Thus, without a word, superbly drenched, they cross the lobby (long since deserted) and take the corridors to their room. Their clothing drips, they tremble with cold, they must change.

And then?

What do you mean, "then"? They will make love, what did you think? That night they will be silent, she will only moan a bit, like a person who has been wronged. Thus everything can go on and the play they just performed tonight for the first time will be repeated in the days and weeks to come. To demonstrate that she is above all vulgarity, above the ordinary world she disdains, she will force him to his knees again, he will blame himself, will weep, she will be all the nastier, she will cuckold him, parade her infidelity, make him suffer, he will fight back, be crude, threatening, determined to do something unmentionable, he will smash a vase, yell hideous insults, whereupon she will feign fear, will accuse him of being a rapist and aggressor, he will refall to his knees, recry, redeclare himself guilty, then she will let him sleep with her and so on and so forth for weeks, months, years, for eternity.

41

And the Czech scientist? His tongue stuck against the loose tooth, he says to himself: This is all that's left of my whole life: a loose tooth and my panic at having to wear a denture. Nothing else? Nothing at all? Nothing. In a sudden flash, his whole past appears to him not as a sublime adventure, rich in dramatic and unique events, but as a minuscule segment in a jumble of events that crossed the planet at a speed that made it impossible to see their features, so much so that maybe Berck was right to take him for a Hungarian or a Pole, because maybe he really is Hungarian, Polish, or maybe Turkish, Russian, or even a dying child in Somalia. When things happen too fast, nobody can be certain about anything, about anything at all, not even about himself.

When I described Madame de T.'s night, I recalled the well-known equation from one of the first chapters of the textbook of existential mathematics: the degree of speed is directly proportional to the intensity of forgetting. From that equation we can deduce various corollaries, for instance this one: our period is given over to the demon of speed, and that is the reason it so easily forgets its own self. Now I would reverse that statement and say: our period is obsessed by the desire to forget, and it is to fulfill that desire that it gives over to the demon of speed; it picks up the pace to show us that it no longer wishes to be remembered; that it is tired of itself; sick of itself; that it wants to blow out the tiny trembling flame of memory.

My dear countryman, companion, renowned discoverer of *Musca pragensis*, heroic laborer on the scaffoldings, I can no longer bear to watch you standing stock-still in the water! You're going to catch your death of cold! Friend! Brother! Stop torturing yourself! Get out! Go to bed. Be happy you're forgotten. Snuggle into the soft shawl of universal amnesia. Stop thinking about the laughter that wounded you—it no longer exists, that laughter, it no longer exists just as your years on the scaffoldings and your glory as a victim of persecution no longer exist. The château is quiet, open the window and the fragrance of the trees will fill your room. Breathe. Those are three-hundred-year-old chestnuts. Their rustle is the same one Madame de T. and her Chevalier heard as they made love in the pavilion that at the time was visible from your window but that you will never see, alas, because it was destroyed fifteen years later, during the 1789 revolution, and all that remains of it is the few pages of Vivant Denon's novella, which you have never read and, very probably, never will.

42

Vincent did not find his undershorts; he slipped his trousers and shirt onto his wet body and set off running after Julie. But she was too nimble and he too slow. He runs through the corridors and sees that she has disappeared. Not knowing how to find her room, he realizes his chances are slim, but he goes on wandering the corridors in hopes that a door will open and Julie's voice will say: "Come, Vincent, come here." But everyone is asleep, there is not a sound to be heard, and all the doors stay shut. He murmurs: "Julie, Julie!" He murmurs louder, he shouts his murmur, but only silence answers. He pictures her. He pictures her face turned diaphanous by the moon. He pictures her ass hole. Ah, her ass hole, which was naked right near him and which he missed, totally missed. Which he neither touched nor saw. Ah, that terrific image is back again, and his poor member awakes, rises up, oh, it rises up, uselessly, senselessly, and immensely.

Back in his room, he slumps onto a chair and has nothing in his head but desire for Julie. He would do anything in the world to find her again, but there is nothing to be done. She will come into the dining room tomorrow morning for her breakfast, but he, alas, will already be back in his office in Paris. He does not know her address, or her last name, or where she works, anything.

"And that imbecile hymn to joy, besides; how can you listen to that?"

"Forgive me. Again it's my imagination's fault."

"What do you mean, your imagination? Are you the person who wrote the Ninth Symphony? Are you starting to think you're Beethoven now?"

"No, that's not what I meant."

"That symphony has never sounded so unbearable, so out of line, so pushy, so childishly grandiloquent, so stupidly, naïvely vulgar. I can't take any more. That's really the last straw. This château is haunted, and I don't want to stay here another minute. Please, let's leave. Anyhow, the sun's coming up."

And she gets out of bed.

44

It's early morning. I am thinking about the last scene in Vivant Denon's novella. The night of love in the château's secret chamber has come to a close with the arrival of the chambermaid, the confidante, who tells the lovers day is breaking.

The Chevalier dresses at high speed, leaves the room, but loses his way in the château corridors. Fearing discovery, he decides to go in the park and pretend to be walking about like someone who is up very early after a good night's sleep. His head still spinning, he tries to figure out the meaning of his adventure: has Madame de T. broken with her lover the Marquis? is she in the process of doing so? or was she only trying to punish him? what is to follow the night that just ended?

Lost in such questions, he suddenly sees before him the Marquis, Madame de T.'s lover. The man has just arrived, and he hurries up to the Chevalier. "How did it go?" he asks eagerly.

The dialogue that follows will finally show the Chevalier what prompted his adventure: the husband's attention had to be drawn off to a false lover, and that role fell to the Chevalier. Not a pretty role, a rather ridiculous role, the Marquis concedes with a laugh. And as if to reward the Chevalier for his sacrifice, he confides a few secrets: Madame de T. is an adorable woman and above all a woman of matchless fidelity. She has only one single failing: her physical coldness.

The two men return to the château to pay the

husband their respects. The latter is cordial with the Marquis but disdainful toward the Chevalier: he suggests that the young man leave as soon as possible, whereupon the genial Marquis offers him his chaise.

Then the Marquis and the Chevalier go to call on Madame de T. At the end of the conversation, at the door, she manages to say a few affectionate words to the Chevalier; these are the last lines as the novella reports them: "Now your love is drawing you back; she who is the object of that love is worthy of it. . . . Farewell, yet again. You are charming . . . Do not set the Comtesse against me."

"Do not set the Comtesse against me": those are Madame de T.'s last words to her lover.

Immediately thereafter, the very last words of the novella: "I climbed into the chaise that stood waiting. I hunted for the moral of that whole adventure, and . . . I found none."

Yet the moral is there: Madame de T. embodies it: she lied to her husband, she lied to her lover the Marquis, she lied to the young Chevalier. It is she who is the true disciple of Epicurus. Lovable lover of pleasure. Gentle protective liar. Guardian of happiness.

45

The story of the novella is told in the first person by the Chevalier. He has no idea what Madame de T. really thinks, and he is himself fairly frugal in speaking of his own feelings and thoughts. The inner world of the two characters remains hidden or half hidden.

When, in the early morning, the Marquis spoke of his mistress's frigidity, the Chevalier could laugh up his sleeve, because she had just proved the opposite to him. But apart from that one certainty he has no other. What Madame de T. did with him—was that routine for her, or was it a rare, even thoroughly unique adventure? Was her heart touched, or is it still intact? Has her night of love made her jealous of the Comtesse? Her final words commending the Comtesse to the Chevalier—were they sincere, or were they simply impelled by a concern for safety? Will the Chevalier's absence make her nostalgic, or will it leave her indifferent?

And as for himself: when early that morning the Marquis had taunted him, he replied with wit, managing to keep the situation in hand. But how did he really feel? And how will he feel as he leaves the château? What will he be thinking about? The pleasure he experienced, or his reputation as a ludicrous whelp? Will he feel like the victor or the vanquished? Happy or unhappy?

In other words: is it possible to live in pleasure and for pleasure and be happy? Can the ideal of hedonism be realized? Does that hope exist? Or at least some feeble gleam of that hope?

46

He is tired to death. He longs to stretch out on the bed and sleep, but he cannot risk not waking up in time. He must leave in an hour, no later. Seated on the chair, he jams the motorcycle helmet down on his head with the idea that its weight will keep him from dozing off. But sitting with a helmet on one's head and being unable to sleep makes no sense. He rises, determined to leave.

The imminence of departure reminds him of Pontevin. Ah, Pontevin! Pontevin will quiz him.

What should he tell him? If he tells everything that happened, Pontevin will be amused, that's for sure, and so will the rest of the crowd. Because it's always funny when a narrator plays a comic role in his own story. In fact, nobody does that better than Pontevin. For instance, when he tells about his experience with the typist he dragged around by the hair because he had got her mixed up with another woman. But watch it! Pontevin is shrewd! Everyone assumes his comic tale is a cover for a truth that is far more flattering. The listeners envy him his girlfriend with her demands for rough treatment, and they jealously imagine a pretty typist he does God knows what with. Whereas if Vincent tells the story of the fake copulation at the edge of the swimming pool, everyone will believe him and laugh at him and his fiasco.

He paces back and forth in the room and tries to edit his story a little, reshape it, add a few touches. The first thing he has to do is transform the simulated coition into a real coition. He imagines the people coming down to the pool, stunned and charmed by the pair's amorous embrace; all undress hastily, some watching them and others imitating them, and when Vincent and Julie see a magnificent collective copulation fully deployed around them, with a fine sense of stagecraft they rise, gaze again for a few seconds upon the romping couples, and then, like demiurges withdrawing after creating the world, they depart. They depart as they came together, in separate directions, never to meet again.

No sooner do those terrible words "never to meet again" go through his head than his member reawakens; and Vincent wants to bang his head against the wall.

Here's a curious thing: while he was inventing the orgy scene, his dreadful arousal had gone away; by contrast, when he evokes the absent real Julie, he is madly aroused again. Therefore he clings to his orgy story, imagines it and tells it to himself over and over: they make love, the couples turn up, watch them, undress, and soon around the swimming pool there is nothing but the heaving of multiple copulation. Finally, after several reruns of this little pornographic film, he feels better, his member is behaving again, nearly calm.

He imagines the Café Gascon, his cronies all listening to him. Pontevin, and Machu grinning his appealing idiot grin, Goujard putting in his erudite remarks, and the others. As a closer, he'll tell them: "I fucked for you, boys, your cocks were all there with me in that gorgeous orgy, I was your proxy, I was your ambassador, your deputy fucker, your cock for hire, I was a plural cock!"

He strides the room and repeats the last phrase several times aloud. Plural cock, what a great find! Then (the disagreeable arousal has already totally vanished) he picks up his bag and leaves.

47

Véra has gone to pay at the desk, and I carry a little valise down to our car in the courtyard. Regretting that the vulgar Ninth Symphony should have kept my wife from sleeping and pre-cipitated our departure from this place where I was so content, I take a wistful look around me. The château's front steps. It was there that the husband, courteous and icy, came to greet his wife, accompanied by the young Chevalier, when the carriage pulled up as the night began. There, some ten hours later, the Chevalier emerges, alone now, with no one for company.

When the door of Madame de T.'s apartment had closed behind him, he heard the Marquis's laughter, soon joined by another laugh, a woman's. For a moment his steps slowed: why are they laughing? are they making fun of him? Then he does not want to hear another thing, and without delay he heads for the exit; yet in his soul he still hears that laughter; he cannot rid himself of it. He remembers the Marquis's remark: "So you don't see how very comical your role is?" When, early that morning, the Marquis asked him that malicious question, he did not blink. He knew the Marquis was cuckolded, and he cheerfully told himself that either Madame de T. was about to leave the Marquis, and so he himself was sure to see her again, or else that she was taking revenge, and so he was likely to see her again (because a person who takes revenge today will take it tomorrow too). That is what he could think just an hour earlier. But now, after Madame de T.'s final words, everything has become clear: the night would have no sequel. No tomorrow.

He leaves the château in the chill morning

emptiness; he tells himself that nothing is left to him of the night he has just lived through, nothing but that laughter: the anecdote will get around, and he will become a joke figure. It is a well-known fact that no woman desires a man who is a joke. Without asking his leave, they have put a jester's cap on his head, and he does not feel up to wearing it. In his soul he hears the voice of revolt urging him to tell his story, to tell it the way it happened, tell it openly and to everyone.

But he knows he will not be able to do that. Becoming a boor is even worse than being ludicrous. He cannot betray Madame de T., and he will not betray her.

48

By another door, a more discreet one near the reception desk, Vincent goes out into the courtyard. He keeps making himself retell the story of the orgy beside the swimming pool, no longer for its anti-arousal effect (he is already very far from any arousal) but in order to blot out the unbearably heartbreaking memory of Julie. He knows that only the invented story can make him forget what really happened. He wants to tell that new story openly and soon, transform it into a ceremonial trumpet fanfare that will render null and void the wretched counterfeit coition that caused him to lose Julie.

"I was a plural cock," he repeats to himself, and in answer he hears Pontevin's conspiratorial laughter, he sees that appealing grin on Machu, who will say: "You're a plural cock, and we'll never call you anything else but Plural Cock." He likes that idea, and he smiles.

As he walks toward his motorcycle, where it is parked at the far end of the courtyard, he sees a man a little younger than he, dressed up in an outfit from long ago and coming toward him. Vincent stares at him, stupefied. Oh, he must be really knocked out after that insane night: he can't come up with any sensible explanation for this apparition. Is it an actor wearing a historical costume? Maybe connected to that television woman? Maybe somebody was shooting some commercial here at the château yesterday? But when their eyes meet he sees in the young man's look an astonishment so authentic that no actor would ever have been capable of it.

49

The young Chevalier looks at the stranger. It is the headgear in particular that catches his attention. Two or three centuries before, chevaliers were supposed to go into battle in helmets like that. But no less surprising than the helmet is the man's inelegance. Long, full, utterly shapeless trousers, the sort only poor peasants might wear. Or monks, maybe.

He feels weary, drained, nearly ill. Perhaps he is asleep, perhaps he is dreaming, perhaps he is delirious. Finally, the man is right in front of him; he opens his mouth and utters a question that confirms the Chevalier in his astonishment: "You're from the eighteenth century?"

The question is peculiar, absurd, but the way the man asks it is even more so, with a strange intonation, as if he were a messenger come from a foreign kingdom and had learned his French at

court without knowing France. It is that intonation, that unbelievable pronunciation, which
made the Chevalier think this man really might
belong to some other period.

"Yes, and you?" he asks.

"Me? The twentieth." Then he adds: "The end
of the twentieth." And he adds further: "I've just
spent a marvelous night."

The remark strikes the Chevalier. "So have I,"
he says.

He pictures Madame de T. and is suddenly
overcome by a wave of gratitude. My God, how
could he pay such mind to the Marquis's laughter? As if the most important thing were not the
beauty of the night he had just spent, the beauty
that still grips him in such intoxication that he is
seeing phantoms, confusing dreams with reality,
feeling himself flung out of time.

And the man in the helmet, with his strange
intonation, repeats: "I've just spent a completely
marvelous night."

The Chevalier nods as if to say, Yes, I know
what you mean, friend, who could understand
you better than I? And then he thinks about it:
he has promised discretion, so he can never tell

anyone what he has experienced. But is an indiscretion still an indiscretion after two hundred years? He has the sense that the god of the libertines has sent him this man just so he can talk to him; so he can be indiscreet while still keeping to his promise of discretion; so he can set down a moment of his life somewhere in the future; project it into eternity; transform it into glory.

"Are you really from the twentieth century?"

"I certainly am, old man. There are amazing things happening in this century. Moral liberation. I tell you, I've just spent a terrific night."

"So have I," the Chevalier says once more, and he prepares to tell him about his.

"A strange night, very strange, incredible," repeats the man in the helmet, his stare heavy with insistence.

The Chevalier sees in this stare the stubborn urge to speak. Something in that stubbornness disturbs him. He understands that that impatience to speak is also an implacable uninterest in listening. Having run up against that urge to speak, the Chevalier instantly loses the taste for saying anything at all, and at once he ceases to see any reason to prolong the encounter.

He feels a new wave of weariness. He strokes his face with his hand and catches the scent of love Madame de T. has left on his fingers. That scent stirs him to nostalgia, and he wants to be alone in the chaise to be carried slowly, dreamily to Paris.

50

The man in the old-time outfit seems to Vincent very young, and thus almost required to take an interest in the confessions of people older than he. When Vincent told him twice "I've just spent a marvelous night" and the other answered "So have I," he thought he'd glimpsed a certain curiosity in his face, but then, suddenly, inexplicably, it switched off, covered over by an indifference that was almost arrogant. The friendly atmosphere that lends itself to confidences lasted scarcely a minute and then evaporated.

He looks at the young man's outfit with irritation. Who is this clown, anyway? Those shoes with the silver buckles, the white tights hugging the legs and buttocks, and all those impossible jabots, velvets, laces, covering and draping the chest. With two fingers he takes hold of the ribbon knotted around the fellow's neck and examines it with a smile meant to parody admiration.

The familiarity of the gesture enrages the man in the old-time outfit. His face clenches, full of hatred. He raises his right hand as if to slap the impertinent fellow. Vincent drops the ribbon and retreats a step. After giving him a look of disdain, the man turns away and walks toward the chaise.

The contempt he spat upon him has plunged Vincent right back into his turmoil. Suddenly he feels weak. He knows he will not tell anyone the orgy story. He will not have the strength to lie. He is too sad to lie. He has only one desire: to forget this night speedily, this entire disastrous night, erase it, wipe it out, nullify it—and in this moment he feels an unquenchable thirst for speed.

His step firm, he hastens toward his motorcycle, he desires his motorcycle, he is swept with love for his motorcycle, for his motorcycle on which he will forget everything, on which he will forget himself.

51

Véra climbs into the car beside me.

"Look, there," I tell her.

"Where?"

"There! It's Vincent! Don't you recognize him?"

"Vincent? The one getting on the motorcycle?"

"Yes. I'm afraid he's going to go too fast. I'm really afraid for him."

"He likes to go fast? He does that too?"

"Not always. But today he'll go like a madman."

"This château is haunted. It will bring everyone bad luck. Please, start the car!"

"Wait a second."

I want to go on contemplating my Chevalier as he walks slowly toward the chaise. I want to relish the rhythm of his steps: the farther he goes, the slower they are. In that slowness, I seem to recognize a sign of happiness.

The coachman greets him; he stops, he brings his fingers to his nose, then he climbs up, takes his seat, huddles into a corner, his legs stretched comfortably before him; the chaise starts, soon he will drowse off, then he will wake, and all that time he will be trying to stay as close as he can to the night as it melts inexorably in the light.

No tomorrow.

No audience.

I beg you, friend, be happy. I have the vague sense that on your capacity to be happy hangs our only hope.

The chaise has vanished in the mist, and I start the car.